## "The maid? She stitched my head?"

"Yes." A quirk of a smile tilted his lips. "She once thought to be a nurse."

"And you held me," she whispered.

His smile disappeared. "No need to look so disturbed. It was necessary to keep you still."

She shook her head on the pillow, not sure what she meant. "I only just came to the realization...."

"It's the laudanum. A few days' rest will, with all hope, see you fully recovered."

"Thank you for all you've done." Her words came soft.

He looked at her in mild surprise. "Of course. I could do no less. I'll leave you to your rest now."

Myrna watched him go, her emotions torn. She disliked her current situation and that Dalton Freed had been the one to aid her—numerous times. But a lifetime of lessons harshly learned taught her not to trust in outward appearances. Her host may behave at present like a harmless lamb, but beneath the genial disguise she still suspected a wolf lurked.

And she would never again become the devourer's prey.

## PAMELA GRIFFIN

loves to write, and her books have entertained readers for over a decade. She is a multipublished, award-winning author, and a six-time winner of the Carol Award. She enjoys research, especially historical, and her stories are set in a wide range of states, countries and eras. With each book, her goal is to entertain with believable, lovable characters and intriguing plots that inspire the reader. She would not be where she is today but for the grace of God, and she gives Him all the glory, dedicating every book to Him. Her family has also been a great help to her in the development of her stories—her dad in providing her with anything needed and putting together her website; her mom, her chief critiquer since book one; and her brother and two sons, significant aids to her in research when asked. She is thankful for every one of them and also to all of her readers.

# PAMELA GRIFFIN

# The Governess's Dilemma

HEARTSONG
PRESENTS

Recycling programs
for this product may
not exist in your area.

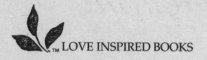 LOVE INSPIRED BOOKS

ISBN-13: 978-0-373-48677-9

THE GOVERNESS'S DILEMMA

But they that wait upon the Lord shall renew their
strength; they shall mount up with wings as eagles;
they shall run, and not be weary;
and they shall walk, and not faint.
—*Isaiah* 40:31

A warm and heartfelt thank-you to my wonderful critique partner, Theo, and to my amazing mother— both are invaluable to me in all they do and the advice and encouragement they give.... For my patient and loving Savior, who taught me how to trust again, a never-ending lesson.

# Chapter 1

1856
*(near Hillsdale, Michigan)*

Myrna stared out the streaked window at the icy particles that swirled past at a frightening speed. She felt as if her own inconstant future mirrored the bleak scene.

Cold. Stark. Perilous and uncertain.

Elizabeth, her young, excitable neighbor until yesterday, had told her with anxious eyes that her life must not be blessed. Elizabeth's mother, Mrs. Flaherty, suggested that the good Lord might be trying to get her attention. Even the affable grocer, Sean, had given his usual quirk of a smile and dollop of advice—that forces beyond her control were taking her on a not-so-merry adventure—as Myrna dug deep into her reticule for the tight wad of dollars to pay off her store credit. Money gained at a steep price, her peace of mind lost in the trade.

Perhaps they were all correct in their conjectures, she

thought with a weary sigh, resting her head against the icy window.

*"Uhhnnnh..."*

The soft murmur of complaint broke into her dismal thoughts and came from the fragile young girl using Myrna's skirts as a pillow. Earlier, Sisi had pulled off her coat, though the railcar was hardly warm, and Myrna used it to cover her. Gently she pushed stray tendrils of light brown curls from the child's damp forehead, finding her skin heated to the touch. She drew her brows together in concern.

Sea-green eyes, a shade lighter than Myrna's, groggily opened.

"Are we there yet?" Sisi asked with a yawn.

Myrna grinned at the endless question again repeated. "I told you, we won't be there till the morning. And likely won't be at our cousin's till the early evening."

Myrna didn't admit she had no idea exactly where their cousin lived, having only an address on a sheet of paper found in her late father's things. But she didn't wish to cause Sisi undue alarm. For being all of seven, the child had endured far more fear and uncertainty than many people three times her age.

"Do you think he'll like us?" Sisi pushed herself up to sit, using Myrna's legs as leverage. The coat slid from her thin shoulders and fell to the bench.

"I'm sure he'll love you, my pet. Who could not?" She tweaked Sisi's nose. This earned her a ghost of a smile, as if Sisi was afraid to let the scrap of happy confidence bloom.

There had been far too many wavering smiles in the past and so many disappointments. It wasn't fair, not one bit, and Myrna silently vowed to do all she could to make Sisi feel safe again. If she must work from the first glimmer of dawn to past the setting of the sun, she would do it. The prospect of meeting a distant cousin and begging for work and a roof over their heads failed to settle well with her McBride pride. But for Sisi, she would grovel in the dirt if she must.

Again she noted the pinched look on Sisi's flushed face. "Are you not feeling well, sweetness?"

"I'm hungry," Sisi complained, holding her tummy.

Myrna wasn't surprised. The bread and cheese Mrs. Flaherty gifted them with before their hurried departure had been devoured long hours ago.

Spotting the flowered hat of the lady who earlier had been selling apples from a basket, Myrna fished a penny from her reticule. "Then we must do something about that. I'll just be a moment," she reassured before rising from her seat and maneuvering the narrow aisle, heading to the front of the train car.

Almost there, she watched a porter move through the door of the attached car. He made eye contact, giving a polite tug of his cap. The mild boredom in his eyes flashed to alarm at the same time the earsplitting screech of metal grinding against metal filled her ears. Rapidly he swung his head around to look.

Terrified, Myrna grabbed the nearest bench seat before whirling to hurry back to Sisi. The gaslights flickered. A stir of hushed voices lifted in alarm. A woman screamed.

The train car jarred with the horrendous force of impact, followed by a distant explosion. Thrown off her feet, Myrna grabbed for a handhold, catching nothing but air. She cried out Sisi's name in the moment before her head smacked against something hard, and her mind went black.

Dalton grabbed the seat before him, unconsciously flinging his free arm sideways in protection against the elderly woman to his left.

The car went dark. Somewhere, a woman screamed,

her panicked words lost in the shrieking and weeping that filled the former gaps of nocturnal silence as the car swayed and careened. Dalton lost his hold, thrown to the aisle. Pain ripped through his upper arm. At last the railcar swung to a slow standstill, landing back on all wheels with a thudding crash. The acrid stench of smoke and flame pervaded his nostrils.

Struggling to curb his fear, Dalton awkwardly sat up. "Are you all right?" he asked the woman, who lay slumped over on his seat. The whirling snow outside the windows provided a muted glow of light. Where it failed to reach, there remained only thick darkness.

The woman gave an abrupt nod, pushing herself up to sit. "I—I think so. My leg is stuck."

That area was in shadow. Dalton could barely see the floor or her skirt to view the damage and attempt to extricate her from the wreckage. He found he was able to move, his legs intact and functional, unhampered by debris. But his left arm throbbed with fire and felt useless. Glancing down, he saw a patch of darkness had soaked through his sleeve. Except for feeling as if he'd been in a fistfight and had come out on the losing side, he felt otherwise unscathed. Yet no matter how he tried, he could not release the woman from her predicament using one arm. She moaned.

"I'll find help." He shivered as a sudden gust of wind hit him. Windows were broken, the freezing air blowing through both sides. From somewhere he heard a man pray in broken syllables for divine intervention.

Dalton carefully stood to his feet. A powerful wave of dizziness threatened to send him to his knees, but he fought it and moved up the narrow passage. The only porter he'd seen recently had been at the front of the car, and he headed that way.

On either side, passengers worked to free themselves

from debris, crying, whispering, taking inventory of their condition. The dark shape of a woman hobbled his way, knocking directly into him. He grabbed her around the waist to stop her when she tried to push past and take him with her in the process.

"Please." Her husky plea came to him from the shadows concealing her face. "I must find Sisi." She put an unsteady hand to her head. In the minimal light, he barely made out a dark streak running down one side of her temple to her cheek. "Sisi, where are you, my pet? Why won't you answer?"

Her voice wavered on a hysterical note and she swayed. Dalton grabbed her by the arms. Her knees gave out and instinctively he brought her close, barely able to hold her up, his injured arm weakened with pain.

"She was sleeping," the young woman went on in a dazed manner against his overcoat. "In my lap. She was hungry, and—and I left her. I never should have left…" Her limbs went slack again, and Dalton tightened his hold around her slender form.

He was surprised about all this commotion over a pet when people were badly injured and in need of immediate aid. She seemed confused, and he wondered if she even knew what she said.

"Sisi *has* to be all right. If she's hurt or—" she let out a pitiful whimper that tore at his heart "—I'll never forgive myself. She didn't want to go, but I had no choice." The woman sobbed and grabbed the lapels of his coat. "You must help me find her!"

"There's a passenger back there with her leg trapped—"

The woman in his arms clutched his coat more tightly and gave it an angry little shake.

"Don't you understand? She's all I have left! She's so small and fragile—*Sisi!*" she called again, breaking free from his hold and managing to step past. At once, she stumbled. He let out a soft exclamation and grabbed her again before she could hit the floor. An apple rolled away from her skirts and under a bench.

"You're wounded, in no shape to search."

"I have to! She's somewhere near—"

"You can barely walk—"

"Please—she's just a child!"

He blinked in startled realization. "Sisi's *a child?*" The passengers he'd seen in their car mostly consisted of men along with a handful of women. He hadn't known children were on board.

"Of course," she snapped, then grabbed her head and groaned. Pressed against him as she was for support, he could feel her entire body tremble.

"All right," he said more quietly. "Don't panic. I'll find her. What does she look like?"

"Brown hair. Blue dress…"

"Stay here." He helped her to sit on the nearest empty seat. *"Don't move,"* he stressed, concerned that she might faint if she tried.

The pale light of winter coming from outdoors now reached her face, and she looked at him with huge, glazed eyes that did not appear to see him. Clearly she needed help. But Dalton was no physician and could only manage what was within his means.

"Sisi!" he called as he retraced his steps down the aisle, kicking aside another apple that almost tripped him. He looked in every niche and corner, repeating her name. Many passengers were being helped or helping others. The beefy, dark-skinned porter took charge, urging people toward the exit. Dalton told him of his trapped seatmate. The man assured him that he would see to the woman, then attempted to steer Dalton toward the exit with the other passengers.

"Not yet," he insisted, pulling away. "I must find some-one first."

Glancing outside, he noted with relief that the heavy snowfall had lifted. Landmarks of the countryside could be seen from the long line of windows. They weren't far from town.

With the train emptier and with less to obstruct his vision, Dalton spotted a strip of blue cloth from beneath a seat where the outside light hit it. His heart dove to the bottom of his chest at the thought that the child might be crushed. He saw a thin leg in a black stocking move and hurried forward.

"Sisi?"

At a soft whimper, relief washed through him. Despite the fiery ache in his arm, he reached for the child, managing to pull her from beneath a bench seat that had broken in the collision and under which she hid. "It's all right," he comforted the tiny girl who powerfully shook in the cradle of his arms. "You're safe."

"Where's Mar-ma?" she whimpered, her voice so soft and groggy he barely understood her. "I want Marma."

"Are you Sisi?"

She gave a jerky nod. A bad bruise covered her left cheek and eye, and her lip was bleeding. But he didn't sense anything in her body broken, and she didn't squirm in great pain as if it was.

"Do you hurt anywhere?"

"My face. And my tummy."

He saw no blood on her dress and guessed there must be bruises beneath. Carefully he stood with her and made his way toward her mother. The woman had vacated the seat where he'd left her and searched the floor in front of it.

"Madam?"

Unsteadily she turned, grabbing the back of the bench seat for balance. In the dim glow, her face brightened.

"Sisi!" She struggled to stand and reached for the child, hugging her even as Dalton held fast.

"We must get off this train." Smoke drifted everywhere, but whether it came from inside or outside he had no clue. "Can you walk?"

"Yes."

The woman followed as he led the way through the darkened interior. They were almost to the exit when she staggered against him.

"Easy," he gently warned. The porter helped them both step down onto snowy ground that reached almost to his knees. Once they trekked a safe distance away, with the woman clutching the back of his coat for balance, he set the child on her feet, afraid he might drop her. His wounded arm ached dreadfully, unable to handle even her slight weight any longer.

Everywhere, passengers stood huddled or sat in the snow, their faces pale with shock, their eyes haunted. Most looked with horrified wonder and confused disbelief at what was left of the train on which many of them had been sleeping until minutes ago. Dalton also turned to observe the devastation.

At a bend in the track, fire leaped from a railway car, near what was left of the mangled engine. Scattered victims lined the area along the length of what remained of the train. Dalton could barely make out shapes in the distance but could see the disaster well enough to realize another train had collided with them head-on.

"Dear God in heaven help us all," he heard his elderly seatmate whisper. He silently added to her prayer for help to arrive soon, relieved to see that the porter had made good on his promise to free the woman sitting beside him.

Dalton had never witnessed such massive destruction. Both locomotives were twisted and broken. Railway cars lay on their sides or at odd angles off the tracks, those closest to the crash having received the worst of the impact as fire from the explosions licked up their metal sidings and shimmered in the darkness. Their car and others toward the caboose remained upright, having received less damage.

At the sound of a child softly crying, Dalton looked back at the woman and her daughter.

With the orange glow from the distant fires illuminating her face, the woman appeared younger than he first thought. Too young to have a child Sisi's age. He placed her at twenty. The child appeared to be a little younger than his niece, who was nine.

Sisi's glassy eyes turned up to him, as if pleading with him to make her world right again.

"Help should arrive soon," he reassured her, placing a gentle hand against the child's head. "The depot isn't far. They would have received word, and telegraphs will spread the news." He found it ironic that a few minutes more and he would have safely disembarked from the train.

The vacant look remained in the woman's eyes.

"You should sit down," he quietly ordered.

Her gaze lowered to his torn sleeve. "You're bleeding."

Dalton looked at his arm. The patch of blood had spread. "It's nothing. I can manage."

She put her hands to her blue scarf and hesitated, as if uncertain what to do, then pulled it loose from her neck. Without a word she wrapped the long strip of wool around his upper arm. Her fingers fumbled, but he uttered no complaint, only stared at her face in curiosity, hardly aware of the increased sting.

She glanced up then quickly down again.

"You helped find Sisi," she offered by way of explanation.

"Your daughter?"

"Sisi is all I have left…" Her words trailed off as she looked back to the wreckage in a daze.

"And your husband? What of him? Was he also on the train?" When she didn't answer, he insisted, "Do you want me to help look for him among the passengers?"

Her eyes slowly flicked up to his. From the sluggish droop of her lids and the blank look she continued to give him, more noticeable up close and with more light, he worried that her injury was far more serious than he had first thought. Head wounds could be severe. Fatal. Blood smeared her auburn hair and pallid skin. She put her hand to her cheek to wipe some away and he noticed the dull flash of a wedding ring.

He pulled a handkerchief from his pocket and wiped the remainder of blood from her face, then lightly blotted it from her temple. His entire kerchief grew red and he frowned.

"Best to hold it there," he instructed.

"No one but Sisi and I were traveling," she said after a moment, as if just remembering his earlier question.

When she remained immobile, he lifted her hand to the wadded kerchief and placed her palm over the cloth. "Keep pressure on it to stop the bleeding. You need to sit down."

She did not resist as he helped her to the frozen ground.

A perfunctory glance at his gold pocket watch showed it was broken, the hands still pointing near midnight. It could have been minutes since the crash; it could have been hours.

At last, the bobbing light of a lantern appeared over a distant hill and a wagon rolled into view. First one, then others came. Dalton blew on his hands, rubbing them together for futile warmth as he waited and watched several citizens of Hillsdale bring blankets and first aid to the survivors. The seriously injured were placed in wagon beds to be taken to town.

"Mr. Freed, sir?"

Taking his concerned gaze off the young woman who

held tightly to the girl, Dalton turned at the welcome sound of a familiar voice.

"Jonas." He clapped a hand to his servant's shoulder. "I cannot tell you how g-good it is to see you." The prolonged cold made his lips stiff and speech difficult.

"Your mother received word of your arrival and sent me to fetch you. It's lucky I made it to the depot before the storm grew bad."

"And quite f-fortuitous that it has now seemed to pass."

"Yes." The short, balding man stared at the wreckage and the fires in disbelief. "Such a terrible tragedy."

"Indeed."

"I'm happy to see you're well, sir. When I heard news of two trains colliding and saw the glow in the sky, I had no idea what to expect. And, well, sir, I also wish to offer my condolences…about your brother."

"Thank you, Jonas."

Dalton had no wish to speak of the terrible misfortune that had forced his return to Eagle's Landing. One tragedy was enough to deal with at a time.

The snow began to fall again, light but steady. He wished for no more than to reach home before a second storm could hit, have his arm tended to and fall into a warm, soft bed.

"The carriage?"

"Just around the bend, sir."

Dalton studied the wooded area. More citizens had arrived to help, but the survivors in need of aid and shelter far outnumbered volunteers. Additional help would likely follow, but the young woman sitting in snow past her hips needed prompt medical attention. Others appeared to be more badly injured than his two charges, as he'd come to consider the woman and her child, and there was no telling how long it would be before either one received aid. They would do better to rely on Genevieve and her remedial

tonics than to wait for Dr. Clark or any of his associates.
And there certainly was room for two more in his carriage.

"Come with me." He crouched down and placed a gentle
hand on the woman's shoulder. Her eyes remained dull
and unresponsive. "I will see to it th-that you and Sisi receive the care you need. My driver is h-here to take us to
my family estate."

To his surprise she snatched her arm from his grasp.
"No."

"No?" He shook his head in bewilderment.

"Sisi and I will stay with th-the others and wait for
help."

"You might have a very long wait." He waved a hand
to include their frozen surroundings and the multitude of
the wounded. "I can offer help now. Su-surely it is best to
remove yourselves from these elements straightaway and
f-find a warm fire? Your daughter has no coat." He motioned to the shivering child in her woolen dress.

"My daughter…" The woman blinked then seemed to
notice the girl's lack of outerwear for the first time. She
winced. "I'll find a blanket." Instead, she fumbled with the
buttons of her own coat, but her fingers shook too much
to be effective.

She had bound and knotted her scarf tightly around his
sleeve or Dalton would remove his long coat for the sake
of the child. "This is utter foolishness," he said in frustration. "Of c-course you'll come with me. I have servants
to provide aid, and you plainly need it."

He picked up the child for the second time that night
and began trudging through the snow, knowing her mother
would follow. The stinging cold made his wound numb
and made it easier to manage the slight burden. At least
Sisi gave no protest.

He heard the awkward shushing of her mother's steps
behind him.

*"Put her down!"*

Dalton turned in surprise at the ferocity in her tone. Witnessing the sudden irrational fear in her flashing eyes, he did as told. Did she think after having done all in his power to help them that he would now cause harm?

The idea provoked his impatience and fueled his irritation.

"Madam, really—"

The rest of his angry protest died on frozen lips as the woman slumped forward in a faint, and Dalton once more caught her in his arms.

# Chapter 2

At the continual rocking motion, Myrna slowly came awake, her head splitting with pain, her entire body feeling bruised. Her cheek rested on something solid and warm. As her awareness cleared, she realized the band of strength around her middle was a man's arm.

Her eyes flew open.

The world lay horizontal.

Myrna blinked to try to gain perspective. Across from her, Sisi slept upright, bundled inside a thick blanket with her legs tucked up beside her and huddled into the corner of a confined, enclosed space. Myrna realized they were inside a slow-moving carriage. The small window at the side provided light from the icy elements. And she also now understood that her head rested on a man's lap, his other hand pressed against her temple.

She jerked to sit upright, breaking free of his hold, and groaned when her head swam with even fiercer pain. Tears filmed her eyes.

"Easy…" His rich tenor came low and calm as he clasped her arm to steady her. She noticed the cloth he held, colored with her blood, and the events of the horrific night came rushing back to add their own torment.

"Where are we?" she asked, moving as far from him as possible on the short leather seat. "Where are you taking us?"

He released a heavy breath. "Keep your voice down, madam. You wouldn't want to wake your daughter after all she's been through."

Myrna glanced at Sisi but did not correct him.

"Perhaps we should start with introductions," he suggested. "I'm Dalton Freed."

She hesitated, knowing it was foolish, but was unable to quench the immediate desire to refuse to reciprocate. "Myrna," she said quietly, barely able to think past the pain. "Myrna McBride."

"I want to assure you, Mrs. McBride, I have only your best interests at heart."

He thought her married, and she remembered the ring and her reason for wearing it.

"You took me against my will," she argued. "I told you I wasn't going with you."

"And I wasn't about to leave you wounded and sitting in the snow when I have the means to help."

"Volunteers had come."

"Yes, and I am one of Hillsdale's citizens, returning home after months away, and equally able to lend my services."

She owed him her gratitude, but once she heard Dalton Freed speak to his driver, she realized he was wealthy. And that changed everything.

A man of affluence had almost destroyed their family. More than once. Twice fooled, doubly foolish. She would not fall into that trap again.

"I appreciate your aid in finding Sisi, but is there no shelter where others have gone? You can take us there."

"When I have the best of provisions and a house with guest rooms? I think not."

"It's what I want."

In the shadowed carriage, she acquired a glimpse of a lean, strong jaw and arresting mouth, which he pulled into a grim line. His eyes flashed and she remembered them to be light gray, like steel. His hair was very dark with a wave to it. That she should remember such details sharpened her unease to be near him.

"It's not only imprudent to take you to a provisional shelter, where it's doubtful either you or your daughter will receive immediate care, but it's also miles behind us. My home is on the outskirts of town. We should be arriving soon. And I have no intention of telling my driver to turn the carriage around. The snow is falling heavily. I want to make it home before another storm can hit."

Myrna glanced at the window, seeing that he was right.

"It seems I have no choice," she whispered.

"You showed no hesitation to receive my help earlier, even begged for it. And suddenly, without reason, you regard me as a ravenous wild beast ready to devour you. Why is that?"

His candid observation held a wry twist, but she sensed an underlying note of hurt.

Sisi stirred. Despite the throbbing in her head, Myrna shifted to the opposite seat. Her actions awkward, she managed to draw Sisi close, slipping her arm around her shoulders and pulling her small head to rest against her side. Sisi's arm looped across her middle. Immediately she fell back asleep.

Aware of Dalton Freed's eyes on her the entire time, Myrna kept her attention fixed to the whirling snow, finding it the least dangerous of her immediate surroundings.

Minutes dragged past in the silence of the carriage, the wind outside keening a lonesome, eerie tune.

The carriage rolled to a stop. Her host-abductor cleared his throat. Myrna jumped so aggressively that she woke Sisi.

"My apologies. I didn't mean to startle you. We have arrived." He opened the door. "Welcome to Eagle's Landing." He stepped out and turned, offering his hand to help her down.

Myrna hesitated before placing her fingers in his large palm, her anxiety escalating to shock when she caught sight of his home. A three-story manor with gables, turrets and chimneys, surrounded on three sides by a forest of tall trees, it surely was the most enormous residence for one man Myrna had seen. She gaped, closing her mouth once he turned from scooping up Sisi. He led the way up several shallow steps and through one of the wide double front doors.

An elderly woman in a black dress and white apron came hurrying to greet him.

"Master Dalton. Welcome home, sir."

"Thank you, Miss Browning. It's good to be home." He sat Sisi on a chair by the entrance table in the large, round foyer. Ahead, a wide staircase followed the wall and wound in an arc to the next level. Everywhere Myrna glanced, she spotted opulence.

"Your hat and coat?" The maid appeared baffled, looking from Myrna, also hatless, to the child without a coat and wrapped in a thick blanket, then back to her employer.

"I lost the hat. The coat will have to stay on awhile longer."

"Sir?"

"A bit of trouble along the way…"

"Dalton, is that you, dear boy?"

At the sound of a mild, well-articulated woman's voice,

Myrna looked with surprise in that direction. He had neglected to tell her he didn't live alone. That realization took the edge off her anxiety, though she could not stop thinking of him as the wicked wolf, due to his earlier comment about comparing him to a wild beast.

A petite woman with upswept dark hair hurried toward him from another room. He stood much taller and had to bend over to receive her hug, reciprocating with one arm.

"It's good to have you home, son. Those trains can be a nuisance, often running late." Her eyes sparkled as she pulled back, then noticed Myrna standing behind him.

"Actually, Mother, there was an accident. As you see, I'm fine," he hurried to reassure her, "but others were not so fortunate."

"An accident?" Dismay knit her brows.

"Two trains. A collision. I brought guests, fellow passengers in need of aid."

Miss Browning gasped at the news, and his mother slowly shook her head.

"Oh, my, how awful. Miss Browning, please find Genevieve."

"Yes, ma'am."

Their words ran together and grew faint. Faces wavered. The entire room began to swim before Myrna's eyes, much like what happened outside the wreckage.

"Dear, are you all right?" Mrs. Freed asked.

"I…" Myrna struggled to remain upright. She clutched the table, putting a hand to her head. "I think I need to sit down." Her legs folded after she got the last words out, and once more she felt his strong arms catch her before she could hit the marble floor.

Dalton swept the injured woman into his arms. Holding her slender form to his chest, he looked with concern at Myrna's white face and closed eyelids. She mumbled something incomprehensible but otherwise did not stir.

"Is she going to be all right?"

At the fearful question, he glanced into the child's anxious eyes. "We'll take good care of her, Sisi. I promise."

"Miss Browning, why don't you take Sisi to the kitchen and give her a slice of pie and some warm milk? Oh, and do tend to the child's poor eye." His mother looked at Sisi with a gentle smile. "Miss Browning will take good care of you. You must be hungry."

The child timidly nodded, and Miss Browning held out her hand. "Come along, then. Let's take care of that shiner first."

"What's a shiner?" Sisi asked, slipping her hand into the housekeeper's and following her out of the foyer.

"That's what you'll be sporting on that eye of yours. Likely you'll be wearing every color of the rainbow."

"I like rainbows."

With Sisi taken care of, Dalton moved up the staircase. "Where should I put her?" he asked his mother who followed at his heels.

"The blue room is always prepared."

At the second landing, he headed to the right and down three rooms, his mother moving ahead to open the door. He strode to the Queen Anne bed and waited for his mother to pull back the blue, lace-trimmed coverlet before setting Myrna down. Her dark lashes fluttered partially open. Upon seeing her alarm, he tried to set her mind at ease.

"It's all right. My mother's here and will take care of you."

She mumbled something that could have been gratitude or refusal—he wasn't sure given his earlier experiences with the woman. Once her head touched the pillow, she closed her eyes again, this time with a slight groan.

Dalton straightened and looked at his mother. "I'll find Genevieve."

"What of your arm?" She approached and touched his sleeve above Myrna's makeshift bandage. "You're hurt! Why did you not say anything? It couldn't have been easy for you to carry her. I could have asked Jonas."

Not for anything would he admit the pain had returned since the shock of the cold had waned. "It's nothing. Others were far more injured than I. Genevieve can look at my arm later."

"I can barely fathom that our family has suffered another accident in so short a time. I don't know what I would have done if I lost you, too."

At the sorrow that clouded her blue-gray eyes, he touched her cheek. "Mother, I will be fine. I'm sorry I wasn't here after..." He paused. "I didn't get your post until two weeks after it happened."

"You're here now." She patted his hand. "But the others! Once the storm lets up, we must send Jonas out with supplies."

He nodded, his eyes on Myrna's unconscious form.

"She's awfully young," his mother said quietly, mirroring his confused thoughts.

"Yes. Too young."

She looked at him oddly. "Whatever do you mean?"

He was given no chance to reply as Genevieve bustled in with her usual shy greeting and took charge of the situation. Seeing he was no longer needed, Dalton retreated to the kitchen.

Sisi sat in the shadows near the kitchen fire, holding a bulky cloth packed with snow to her eye. He took the chair cattycornered to hers and smiled, hoping to reassure her. The housekeeper set a plate of pie before the child then stirred the milk to warm it, giving a cup to Sisi.

"That needs tending to, Master Dalton."

He grimaced at his arm but nodded, allowing Miss Browning to remove the tightly wound and knotted scarf. At last, he took off his coat, damp from snow. She grabbed shears and cut his bloody sleeve, ripping it to gain access to his injury. Miss Browning doused a cloth with cooking sherry, and he hissed as she swabbed what he could now see was a long, deep cut that again bled freely. The searing pain in his arm made his eyes water, and he clenched his jaw, struggling not to groan in front of the child. He concentrated on other things to try to take his mind off the pain, and wondered what in the wreckage could have caused such an injury. He supposed it should be stitched, but only Genevieve had the capability. He hoped the young woman's head wouldn't need to be sewn, though recalling the gash at her temple it was likely. Likely, too, that she had suffered a concussion, having swooned twice.

"Does it hurt much?" Sisi whispered, breaking into his thoughts.

He managed a tense smile. "Does yours?"

"My eye mostly, but not my tummy anymore."

"That's good. Perhaps you just needed to eat."

She took another bite of the quickly disappearing slice. "I like mince pie. Mama used to make it for me when I was good."

"Well then, you deserve it. You were very brave tonight. I'm certain you made your mother proud."

"Mama's in heaven with the angels, but I try to be brave."

At her wistful words, Dalton blinked in confusion. "But I thought—"

"Uncle Dalton! You're home!"

At the eager shriek that pierced the quietude of the kitchen, Dalton winced. Miss Browning spun around from where she stoked the fire.

"Mercy, Rebecca, you'll wake the dead," she admonished. "What are you doing up this time of night?"

Dalton turned to greet his niece, who flew at him in her long, white nightgown and pounced on him where he sat. At least Miss Browning had bandaged his arm before he was tackled.

"Rebecca!" she chided. "Where are your manners, child?"

"That's all right," Dalton reassured the child, pulling her the rest of the way up onto his lap.

She looped her arms around his neck, holding her wrist, and regarded him gravely. "I'm glad you're finally home. Papa went to heaven 'cause of his horse. Did you know?"

He winced. "I know, sugar."

"The horse had to be put down. It was my birthday, but Nana says he's happy now 'cause he's with Mama. I miss Papa awfully." She cast her soulful eyes to the shadowed corner then tilted her head with curious interest. "Hello. Who are you?"

"Sisi," the girl fairly whispered.

"What happened to your face?"

"The train broke."

"Oh." Rebecca regarded her. "Billy Newton was in a fight with a boy at school. His eye looked like yours. It was different colors every day."

Miss Browning approached and fisted her hands on her hips. "You do realize it's gone past three in the morning, missy? What has you up? You should be in bed. The lot of us should."

"It's too noisy. I was sleeping and heard someone scream. Can I have some pie?"

"Tomorrow, you may have pie. For now, you may go to bed."

Dalton wondered if Myrna had issued the scream.

Downstairs, in this wing of the house, it was impossible to hear anything going on above.

Miss Browning smiled at Sisi. "If you're finished, young miss, you should get some sleep, too. Rebecca, take her to your room. She can stay the night with you."

The glum expression at being denied the treat left his niece's face. She crawled down from Dalton's lap and approached Sisi. "You can sleep with me in my bed. I'll let you hold one of my dollies if you like. I got a new one for my birthday. A pony, too, only he came the week before my birthday. I'm nine. How old are you?"

"Seven." Sisi slipped from her chair and set the cold compress on the table, her face now visible in the firelight.

"Ooo, your eye looks like Loretta's new party dress. It's black and violet—it's a pretty dress," Rebecca quickly assured her. "It's got silver stripes, too, only your eye doesn't have any silver around it."

Dalton wearily followed the two little girls to the landing, intending to find rest in his own bed. He hoped his talkative niece would allow their guest her slumber.

His mother met him at the foot of the stairs. After a kiss for her granddaughter and soft words to both girls to sleep well, she looked at Dalton.

"How is your arm?"

He flexed his hand. "Well enough. Miss Browning cleaned and bandaged it. Rebecca said she heard someone scream."

"Yes, that's why I came looking for you." His mother glanced over her shoulder at the children, who were already two-thirds up the staircase and out of earshot. "Genevieve is attempting to sew the cut, but the patient won't hold still. She's barely alert but keeps fighting us. I need to ask Miss Browning if she knows where that dab of laudanum is that Dr. Clark left. But we still need you to hold her. Unless you prefer that I find Charles."

"No, I'll do it."

He could not explain what he failed to understand, but Dalton felt responsible for Myrna and the girl, even if Sisi was *not* her daughter.

And Myrna had allowed him to go on believing the misconception.

Dalton frowned.

*Why?*

Rolling up his undamaged sleeve, Dalton followed his mother upstairs.

Time for explanations must come later. In the present, the welfare of their injured guests came first.

# *Chapter 3*

Myrna had never been hit in the head with a hammer, but if she had, she thought the pain would be tantamount to what she now felt. Her temple throbbed, and she vaguely remembered being restrained by strong arms as someone she had never before seen worked a needle in and out of her skin. She had screamed in fearful anguish, but blissfully had been given a tincture that put her into instant slumber.

She opened her eyes and stared at the ceiling, not daring to move her head on the pillow and make the burning throb worse.

At the bustle of skirts she flicked her eyes to the right to see. A maid gathered items onto a tray and turned. She started in surprise upon seeing Myrna staring at her.

"Oh! I didn't realize you were awake. I'll fetch the mistress."

"Wait!" Myrna groaned when she spoke too loudly, causing painful reverberations inside her head.

"I *am* sorry. 'Tis likely you'll have a splitting headache for some time. I can bring you tea with mint to help."

Myrna fought back the pain. "Sisi, the girl who came with me. Is she all right?"

The young maid's cherry cheeks bunched up in a smile. "Right as rain, that one. She had a wee sniffle the first day, but the lot of us nursed her to health before she could get badly ill."

The girl bore a European accent, somewhere between Irish and British, and Myrna realized how much she missed hearing that lyrical manner of speaking—so similar to the lilt of her Irish-born parents. The maid's words materialized in her mind.

"The first day?"

"You've been lying abed for two days, madam."

Myrna winced at the inappropriate salutation, her thumb brushing the inside of the ring. The girl must have seen it and assumed that she was married, or perhaps the master of the house told her. A hint of guilty remorse nagged at her conscience for withholding the truth, but she knew nothing about these people—and certainly nothing about *him*. She knew only that she was trapped inside his palatial home, for however long it took to recover.

The maid opened the door to leave.

"Oh—good afternoon, sir." The girl's voice became almost giddy. "I was just seeing to Mrs. McBride about fetching her some tea."

"Yes, you do that, Genevieve."

The rich, warm sound of his voice sent a cool shiver down Myrna's spine. Despite the pain, she raised herself a little to see, pulling the thick coverlet up to her neck.

He moved to the foot of her bed and gave a stiff, courteous nod. "Mrs. McBride. I trust you are receiving all that you need?"

"Yes, thank you. I want to see Sisi."

"In due course." He walked to the window and she followed him with her eyes. Pulling aside the heavy drape, he looked out the pane. "Your *sister* is taking luncheon with my niece at the moment."

She didn't fail to notice his slight emphasis on their relationship. Perhaps it had been foolish to let him go on thinking Sisi was her daughter, but from what little she remembered, he arrived at his own conclusions. She had simply never corrected them.

She also never told him she had a husband, not that she could recall; the night of the collision and anything said then was vague. To ward off unwelcome interest from predatory men she wore the ring. Nearly twenty and unattached, she needed it for protection while she was on her own. She'd ignored the prickle of unease that told her she should not mislead *this* particular man, that he was not so easily fooled.

A ravenous wild beast…isn't that what he likened himself to in the carriage? To her way of thinking, a wolf described him well.

In the bright glow of the room's gas lamps, with the partial illumination of daylight from the parted curtains, Myrna got her first true look at the man who had insisted she and Sisi come to his home. His elegant black waistcoat covered wide, powerful shoulders and reached to the middle of his long, trim legs. He turned to look at her, snapping her from her introspection.

"Have you nothing to say?"

Even from the distance of several feet, his eyes seemed to glow, their color under his dark brows such a pale gray they appeared silver, like the intricate whorls of threads in his vest. Gleaming hair, a rich burnished color near black, had been swept from his forehead and grew long, resting just below his high collar. His features she would describe as proud, like his bearing—a long, straight nose, firm, stubborn chin, perfectly shaped lips, the bottom curve a tad fuller than the top; the corners now tilted in a wry, hard twist.

She swallowed hard.

Yes. *Wolf* was the perfect name for him.

Dangerous.

"I would like to see my sister," she said on the edge of a whisper.

His thick brows raised in polite mockery. "So you admit that she *is* your sister."

"I never stated otherwise."

"I called her *your daughter* numerous times, yet you said nothing."

"Please." She put a hand to her head and the bandage there. "I cannot speak of this now."

The stony look left his eyes. A trace of sympathy softened his features.

"My apologies. I should not have confronted you so soon, with you barely recovered from the ordeal. And I know your mind was muddled when first we met. I will leave you to your rest." He moved toward the door then stopped and faced her again. "Is there anyone we should contact? Your husband, perhaps? Jonas is going into town with more supplies for the victims and can send a telegraph then."

She would need to contact her cousin soon. She had sent a wire before leaving St. Clair, to let him know to expect them, but gave no exact date of their arrival, unaware of it at the time. Yet she certainly couldn't share that with Mr. Freed.

"I would prefer to see to that myself, once I've recovered."

He looked at her oddly. "Very well."

Before he could quit the room she spoke. "Please—I... I cannot recall much of that night. Can you tell me what happened?"

His manner became grim. "A mail train hit us on a curve, its headlamp out, but both trains were running blind due to the storm. It is likely that no one will ever know the details, but I suspect neither saw the other coming until it was too late. If then."

Myrna stared in horrified shock. "Was anyone killed?"

"To date, three men were killed outright, three so badly injured they might yet die."

"Oh, dear." Her heart wrenched in sympathy for the injured and those families affected. The fiery ache in her head seemed trivial in comparison.

"We can consider ourselves most fortunate, Mrs. McBride. Death has a habit of choosing its victims without reason and often with callous disregard."

He spoke as if having just experienced the occurrence.

"Were any of those men friends of yours?"

"No. Those who died and lie near death worked on the trains. I never knew them. I should tell you that the baggage car was incinerated in the collision. Everything was consumed."

Myrna dropped her gaze to the coverlet.

People dead. Badly wounded. Possessions lost...

On the train was all she could carry. But it was no great loss. A ratty carpetbag with a change of clothes for her and Sisi and a few personal items easily replaced. The previous week, she had sold her mother's wedding pearls, earrings and a brooch to a greedy pawnbroker, even if it felt like a betrayal to her mother's memory. The heirlooms accrued just enough to pay off the landlord and the grocer, and to buy train tickets. Only her father's pocket watch remained, safely tucked inside her coat pocket, just as her mother's simple wedding band circled Myrna's finger. Anxiously she brushed it with her thumb.

"My mother sent a note with Jonas to ask a physician to come and examine you when one becomes available," the wolf went on. "Genevieve did the best she could, but we would prefer a doctor's opinion."

"Genevieve…" Her eyes grew round with shock. "The *maid? She* stitched my head?"

Faces had been blurry, but at the recurring memory of strong arms around her, Myrna's heart gave a little jump.

"Yes." A quirk of a smile tilted his lips. "Don't be fooled by age. She's young but wise in how to administer medical aid. She once thought to be a nurse."

"And you held me," she whispered.

His smile disappeared. "No need to look so disturbed. It was necessary to keep you still."

"Of course. I didn't mean to imply—" she shook her head on the pillow, not sure what she meant "—I only just came to the realization. Everything is still hazy. I wonder if I'll ever recall all of it."

"It's the laudanum. A few days' rest will, with all hope, see you fully recovered."

"Thank you for all you've done." Her words came soft.

He looked at her in mild surprise. "Of course. I could do no less. I'll leave you to your rest now."

Myrna watched him go, her emotions torn. She disliked her current situation and that Dalton Freed had been the one to aid her—numerous times. But he *had* helped and she would be petty not to acknowledge his kindness. However, it did not alter her opinion of his character. A lifetime of lessons harshly learned taught her not to trust in outward appearances. Her host may behave at present like a harmless lamb, but beneath the genial disguise she still suspected a wolf lurked.

And she would never again become the devourer's prey.

\* \* \*

Dalton stared out the library window at the expanse of countryside frozen in white. His arm ached less now, the threads Genevieve had sewn in little more than a nuisance now.

The prospect of the future loomed dismal, uncertain, and he had left his brother's former study overwhelmed by others' expectations. He feared his shoulders were not wide enough to bear such a burden.

Father had devoted most of his time to Roger, to prepare his eldest to take over the family business and oversee the estate once he inherited that right. Roger had been thirty, nearly eight years older than Dalton when the unforeseeable happened. And now Dalton was head of the household and responsible for the welfare of all who resided within.

He ran tense fingers through his hair and held it bunched at the nape before dropping his arm back to his side. Roger's penmanship never had been neat, but the account books for the estate and his notes on various businesses were practically undecipherable. After Roger's wife died bearing their stillborn second child, Dalton's brother took a downward spiral, and he began to drink his after-dinner brandy all through the day to drown the pain. Before he had left Eagle's Landing six months ago, Dalton tried to sit down and reason with his brother, but Roger would hear none of it. Now Rebecca was an orphan and the entire family might suffer due to Roger's incompetence.

The sound of faint giggling in the corridor brought him out of his dour musings. He turned and mustered a smile for his niece and her new little friend who entered the room. Four days in their home, and the child had shown a remarkable improvement, the blackness having faded around her eye to a dull green and yellow. She stared in wonder at the tall scrolled bookcases of mahogany that filled the library.

He nodded to the children. "Rebecca. Sisi. What brings you girls here?"

"Sisi said she's never seen a liberry with hundreds and hundreds of books."

"Ah." He lifted his brows with a smile at his niece's typical enthusiasm. "Do you read, Sisi?" He asked the question, doubtful of a positive response. To his surprise, the girl nodded.

"My sister teaches me."

"Does she?"

"Only Myrna doesn't have so many books. Only three. And I have trouble with lots of the words."

At mention of the woman lying upstairs in the blue room, Dalton felt a tickle of interest to know more. "Is your sister a teacher?"

Sisi shook her head no.

"A scholar, then?"

"I don't know what that is."

"Does she go to school?"

"Unh-unh. We were going to my cousin's home."

"Oh." Dalton regarded her kindly. "Is that where you two were headed on the train?"

The child nodded, and a glimmer of somber remembrance shone in her eyes. "I don't want to go there anymore."

The fear in Sisi's near whisper tugged at his heart. He had no business interfering, but after all the child had suffered, he wished only to relieve her immediate terror.

"Perhaps you might not have to go by train," he reassured.

"It's the only way. Myrna said so."

"Well, perhaps your sister's husband can be persuaded to come and collect you by some other mode of transport."

She tilted her head with its mop of brown ringlets. "Huh?"

Dalton grinned. "Your sister could contact the man she married to come here. Were you meeting him at your cousin's?"

She covered her mouth and giggled. "Myrna's not married to a husband."

"Not married...?" His words trailed off in confusion. "Of course she must be. Your sister's husband would become your family by marriage. Your brother-in-law."

"I don't have one of those, either." The child glanced toward the door then back at Dalton. "I'm not supposed to tell," she whispered nervously. "Myrna said I mustn't tell a soul about our family. Ever. But you're nice. Will she be angry with me for telling you?"

"Your sister's nice, too," Rebecca said. "She won't be angry. Uncle Dalton can keep a secret." She flashed him a warm smile and grabbed Sisi's hand. "Come, there's something else I want to show you!"

Standing motionless in shock, Dalton watched the girls hasten away in a flurry of hushed whispers and giggles.

After a time, he swiveled back to the window, clasping his hands behind him, his mind a chaotic whirlwind of thought, his heart a violent force of emotion. At the sudden knowledge that he was no longer alone, Dalton turned his attention to the entrance.

The object of his angry speculation wavered at the door.

"Ah, *Mrs. McBride.* How good to see you up and about. I trust you are feeling much improved?"

She hesitated at the threshold. "Yes. I'm looking for Sisi. A servant saw her come to the library."

"She was here. My niece is giving her a tour of the manor."

"Oh. Thank you."

Before she could make a swift retreat, he stepped forward.

"Madam, a moment, if you would be so kind. I have a

matter I wish to discuss." He swept his hand to the side, motioning to one of two wingback chairs by the fire that blazed inside the hearth.

She glanced at the chair like a wary rabbit to a trap. "I should go find Sisi…."

"Please." He struggled to maintain a polite demeanor. "This won't wait. And close the door behind you. I have no wish for our conversation to be overheard."

Cautiously she did as instructed and walked a wide circle around him to take a seat in the chair. Dalton regarded her with cold suspicion the entire time.

He had taken this woman into his home as a victim but now must consider the safety of his family, and evidently she'd been playing quite the masquerade! But to what purpose? Was she a felon wanted by the law? Or perhaps she had committed a crime of which no one knew?

The gloves of refined decorum were coming off. It was time for the truth, and she would not leave this room until he acquired answers.

He slowly moved to stand before her.

She looked up at him in undisguised alarm.

## Chapter 4

Myrna warily observed her host. Despite the flash of suspicious determination in his steel-colored eyes, she resolved to remain calm in the mystery of his anger.

"Very well." She spoke quietly and straightened her spine. "What is it you wish to discuss, Mr. Freed?"

He narrowed his eyes then walked over to the hearth and stared into its dancing flames, clasping his wrist behind him. "I spoke to your sister. She is terrified to resume your journey to your cousin's by train. I suggest you send a telegram to your husband and explain matters, perhaps take an alternative mode of travel."

Myrna clasped her hands more tightly in her lap at his mention of her cousin and the realization that Sisi told him of their plans.

"Yes, thank you, I'll tend to that."

He turned his head sharply to look at her. "You wish to send a telegram to your husband, then?"

Was that not the point of this conversation?

"Yes, if you would please see to it for me, I'll compose the missive…" Her words faded as he again approached and stood before her, his manner intimidating.

"That might be difficult to execute," he clipped, "since you have no husband."

*Oh, Sisi, what have you done?*

"I *do* have a cousin."

"And is *he* your husband?"

"No. But I fail to understand why my personal status should matter."

She twirled her mother's wedding ring around her finger. He caught her nervous act, his jaw set like stone. Grabbing the arms of her chair, he leaned down to her level. Myrna pushed herself back into the cushion in startled surprise. His eyes burned like flint.

"I have no interest in your personal status, Miss McBride, only that you lied."

"I didn't lie," she countered with the same soft brusqueness. "Keeping the truth silent by omission is not a lie."

His short laugh came without amusement. "And the token of gold circling your finger? What does that suggest, if not a lie?"

"Protection!"

"From whom?" he insisted.

She pressed her lips together. He scrutinized her up and down.

"Are you a thief?"

"Wha…" She blinked, caught off guard. "No, of course not!"

"And why should I believe you?" His gaze again lit on the ring. "Perhaps you're wanted by the authorities for criminal activities. Are you using Eagle's Landing as your hideaway?"

"You invited me to stay here while I recover!"

"While blind to the truth of your situation. Unaware of all the facts."

Myrna had endured enough of his bullying. Indignant, she wrapped her hands around the chair arms, close to his, and pushed herself up to sit so that she was level with his eyes. He drew back a fraction in astonishment as she scorched him with her own fire.

"If you recall, I never wanted to come here after the accident. Believe what you will, but I'm a moral, decent woman, Mr. Freed."

"Moral, decent women don't fabricate a pretense to fool others."

"They do if they wish to survive in this merciless world!" She curbed that thought, not wishing to speak to him of such things. "Can you truly blame me? You swept me away after I told you I wouldn't go with you. I woke to find myself at your mercy."

"I said I wouldn't harm you."

"And why should I have believed *you?* You're nothing but a stranger. I couldn't trust you, not after you whisked Sisi and me to your home without my permission and contrary to my wishes. *I didn't ask* to come here."

"Had I left you there, *you might still* be lying in a crude shelter awaiting medical care!"

The sound of giggling, instantly stifled, made them both turn their heads. The door stood open, both children having come to a sudden halt upon witnessing their quiet argument.

Her pitiless interrogator swiftly moved to stand, stepping away from her.

"Rebecca, what have you been told about closed doors and knocking to let anyone inside know that you wish to enter?"

"I'm sorry, Uncle Dalton." Her remorse lasted only seconds before her face lit up. "I was showing Sisi the room the maids prepared for her."

"Myrna, you must see," Sisi exulted, both girls fluttering into the room. "It's bigger than any room at the tenement. It has three long windows and a seat in a round wall to look outside. And the bed and curtains have tassels! Oh, come and see!"

Myrna could hardly refuse as Sisi clutched her arm and pulled, trying to hasten her progress. Not that she wished to remain. She welcomed any excuse to leave Dalton Freed's surly company and gave him no further attention.

Myrna watched the children hurry ahead, hand in hand, a new bounce to her sister's steps. She regretted that Sisi could not always enjoy the benefits of living in such a household, with a playmate her age. But after the harrowing confrontation with its master, Myrna was even more determined to leave the moment she was well enough to do so.

They encountered Miss Browning coming downstairs. The housekeeper regarded Myrna as she might one of the children, had they been naughty.

"Mrs. McBride, the doctor said complete bed rest for one week."

"I only came downstairs to find my sister."

The housekeeper took Myrna by the arm and moved with her up the staircase. "And the mistress will have my head if she knew you were up and about."

Resigned to obeying, though she felt fine, Myrna accompanied the husky older woman to the room she'd been given, and allowed herself to be tucked into the huge bed like a child. Once she left, Myrna asked Sisi to remain. Rebecca lingered, as if uncertain whether to stay or go.

"I'll look at your room another day," she promised Sisi. "Would you bring me a book? Be sure to knock on the door first."

"What book?" Sisi looked overwhelmed with the task. "There's so many."

"Mama had a book she liked," Rebecca said. "Do you want that one?"

"Yes, thank you." At this point, she certainly wasn't picky. "That sounds lovely."

Over the next few days, Myrna regretted her answer.

The gripping novel by Currer Bell was different than anything she'd read, intriguing in a bizarre fashion. She could not help equate Thornfield Hall with Eagle's Landing and the mysterious and dour Mr. Rochester to the character of her intractable host. With no company save for Sisi to share dinners with and the occasional servant to tend her, Myrna dwelled on her current predicament and noted disturbing similarities to the unfolding story of the hapless governess Jane Eyre. A work of fiction, yes, but the novel emphasized her own wretched station in life. While grateful for the Freeds' kindness, she felt a burning need to leave before anything could happen.

Finally, her recovery was deemed complete. But when she visited the bedroom with the turret window to find Sisi, she discovered the chamber empty.

"Sisi?"

She peeked into adjacent rooms, their doors left open, all of them empty. Downstairs, a glance into the dining room and parlor showed no servants in sight. She didn't feel comfortable searching the grand house, intruding where she had no consent, especially after *he* had called her a thief.

One room remained on the main level, and she hastened down its corridor, hoping to find Sisi there. At the closed doors, she hesitated, sensing that her absentminded sister would not have shut them. Fighting back the recollection of her last encounter within this deceptively cozy chamber, she took a steadying breath and knocked on the polished mahogany.

Dalton sat near the hearth fire and tried to make sense of the erratic scrawl that composed his brother's notes. A tapping reached his ears, so faint, he first thought he imagined it. When the sound came again, he straightened and looked at the door. "Come," he instructed, expecting Rebecca, though she was usually boisterous in her entrances.

To his surprise, Myrna approached then came to a stop, her attention flitting to the crackling fire and back to him as if recalling their last encounter there. He had issued a genial farewell to her earlier that morning, never expecting to see her again. Noting her agitation with how she twisted the ring she still foolishly wore, he grew alert, set his book down and rose to his feet.

"Is there a problem, Miss McBride?"

"I cannot find Sisi."

He looked at the mantel clock. "Jonas should return from town within the hour. Your train doesn't arrive till half past. There's plenty of time."

She didn't look convinced. "Perhaps she's with Rebecca?"

Since the two children had been practically joined at the hip upon Sisi's arrival to Eagle's Landing, Dalton deduced her assumption an accurate one.

"Please, if you don't mind," she continued, "will you ask a servant to help me search?"

Genuine worry filled her eyes. No matter how he felt with regard to her possible nefarious activities or feeble excuses for them, it unnerved him to see any woman approach a state of panic.

Crossing the distance between them, he noted her sudden wary expression.

"I'll help you find her," he said quietly.

Surprise then gratitude lit her eyes and she nodded.

A search of the lower floor yielded no results, save for the downstairs maid, Gladys, who he told to check the kitchen area. They retraced their steps to the main staircase and met Jonas exiting the foyer. Dalton reached for his pocket watch and flipped it open, the crack on the glass reminding him it was broken. He grimaced and slipped the useless item back in its pocket.

"Mr. Freed, Miss McBride." Jonas nodded to each. "It's soon time to leave for the depot, sir. Straight up on the hour."

"Have you seen Rebecca or Sisi?" Dalton asked.

"No, sir. We only just returned."

"And Mother?"

"She went to the conservatory. Said she wished to be alone."

Dalton frowned, having just learned that morning of her friendship with one of the newly widowed victims of the train collision. A sensitive soul, his mother in all likelihood had been deeply affected by the woman's pain, though knowing her, she would have only shown strength when she went to visit the poor soul. And although she hid it well, she was still mourning Roger's death, in her own resilient way. His mother needed rest.

"Thank you, Jonas. If you would search the stables for the girls? Ask Charles to search the grounds."

The man nodded and left.

"You don't think they would have gone outside, in the snow?" Myrna followed him up the staircase.

"I rule nothing out. Rebecca hasn't visited the stables in weeks, but that was before your sister arrived. She might wish to show off her new pony. If we find Sisi within the next fifteen minutes, there will still be time to get you to the station." Recalling the disastrous images of fire and broken, twisted metal as far as the eye could see, he was surprised it had taken workers only a week to clear the tracks.

Together they swept the second landing. With one room left, Dalton hesitated, his hand at the knob.

"If they're not in here, they're not on this floor."

"The third floor, perhaps?"

"We no longer use that floor, save for storage."

Myrna withheld a challenging reply that such a forbidden locale might be the first place wayward children would go. He gently cupped her shoulder, and she looked up in startled question. His eyes no longer seemed hard like metal but glistened softly, inviting her trust.

"Do not be troubled. We will find your sister."

She nodded faintly, and he opened the door.

Clearly the family no longer used this room, either. White dust cloths shrouded furniture, with the bed the only item naked to the eye and stripped of all linens, leaving a bare mattress.

Dalton remained on the threshold. A pained expression crossed his features, his mouth taut as he glanced about the bedchamber. Myrna noticed the pattern on the faded, papered walls bore little blue cornflowers.

"Did this room belong to Rebecca's mother?" The curious words slipped out before she could hinder them.

"No." He narrowed his eyes at a corner of the room. "There."

At his low instruction, Myrna looked to see a sheet that appeared to cover a small table. In the stillness of the room the cloth fluttered slightly, as though stirred by a nervous foot.

Dalton covered the area in several rapid strides and whipped the dust cloth away. Both girls shrieked. Myrna hurried up beside him, bending to see. Sisi and Rebecca sat huddled beneath a small desk, in its cubbyhole, their arms wrapped around each other. Both girls shrank closer to the wall.

"Uncle Dalton, you're suppose' to knock before entering a room," Rebecca petulantly chided.

"You're in enough trouble, young lady, without correcting your elders," he said sternly. "Come out from there at once. You know you're not allowed in this room!"

"Sisi, that goes for you, too," Myrna added.

"I don't wanna go!" Tears trembled in Sisi's voice. "Don't ever wanna ride a train again. Please don't make me, Myrna!" She buried her face against Rebecca's shoulder and sobbed. "I like it here...."

"We cannot stay." Myrna calmed her tone upon seeing how upset Sisi truly was. "Come now, enough of this. Our cousin is expecting us."

"No!" Sisi insisted. *"I won't go!"*

Myrna blinked, uncertain how to respond. Sisi misbehaved at times, usually to become quickly reconciled. Never did she act out with such rebellion and emphatic desperation. Dalton showed no similar hesitance as he grabbed his niece by the ankles and pulled.

"No—Uncle Dalton—don't!"

Her pleas met deaf ears as he hauled the girl to her feet.

"Go to your room, Rebecca. *Now,*" he added, pointing to the door when she hesitated.

She looked from Sisi to Dalton, undecided, then scurried from the room. Sisi drew into a tight ball, shrinking farther away, her teary eyes full of mistrust. Dalton looked at Myrna in question, silently asking permission to retrieve her as he'd done with his niece. Myrna shook her head no.

"Sisi," she tried again, keeping her voice soft. "You cannot stay under that desk forever."

"If I come out, you'll make me go on the train," Sisi whimpered.

"It's too late for that now." Even without consulting her

father's pocket watch, Myrna knew more than fifteen minutes had elapsed since they spoke to Jonas.

"Promise? I don't have to ride the train?"

Myrna sighed. "You don't have to ride the train *tonight*." She held out her hand. "Come now, Sisi. We mustn't bother Mr. Freed any longer, and you shouldn't be sitting on that cold floor. You're fortunate you didn't get deathly ill when you stood in the snow without your coat...."

Tentatively Sisi placed her hand in Myrna's, and Myrna helped her trembling sister crawl out from her place of concealment and stand. Before Myrna could again speak, Sisi whirled to face their host, clasping her hands beneath her chin.

"Oh, please let us stay, sir." Sisi stunned Myrna further when after a moment's hesitation, she catapulted into Dalton, throwing her arms around his waist. "I'll be good! I promise. Can't I stay and be your niece, too? I never had an uncle." She lifted her tear-streaked face to look at him. With his arms still hanging at his sides in shock, he stared at Sisi then Myrna, clearly at a loss for words.

Myrna was the first to recover. "Sisi, go to your room. You may take your meal there and stay there the rest of the night." She couldn't send her to bed without supper, Sisi's health being a frequent concern. Neither could she let her wayward conduct go unpunished.

Her sister pulled back from Dalton and sheepishly hung her head.

"I'll be in soon. And Sisi, go directly to your room. No stopover to see Rebecca."

"Yes, Myrna."

Once Sisi left, Myrna turned her attention to Dalton.

"I apologize. She's not usually so forward. She's actually quite timid around strangers." Myrna added the last in confusion. "I suppose she feels comfortable with you since you rescued her from the train." Saying the words made her uneasy. The last thing she wanted was to think of Dalton Freed as their savior, even if he *had* rescued them. "We'll leave tomorrow."

He nodded. "I'm not upset. The experience last week terrorized her."

"Yes, well, I'll talk to her. Thank you for your help." Myrna nervously gripped a fold of her skirt. "I hope we haven't been too much of an imposition."

"No, you haven't been an inconvenience."

An awkward moment stretched longer. Myrna found it difficult to look away from his compelling silver eyes. He did nothing to break the contact.

She cleared her throat. "I should go."

"Yes." He stepped back.

She realized he waited for her to precede him and left the room.

Upon hearing the door click shut, she turned her head to see that the corridor stood empty and he remained inside the forgotten chamber.

A curiosity, certainly, but Myrna desired no further intrigues for one night and hastened away before he could open the door and catch her there staring.

# Chapter 5

Deciding to delay her discussion with Sisi, Myrna went downstairs to seek the cook and ask that she prepare a tray. She took a corridor, hoping it would lead to the kitchen. Coming abreast of one room, its door ajar, a lovely melody from within made her pause.

A peek inside revealed the mistress of the house sitting at a grand piano. At the sudden wash of light from the doorway in the otherwise dimly lit parlor, the woman looked up in surprise and turned her head. Myrna froze at being discovered.

"I apologize. I was looking for the cook and heard the music."

Before she could close the door she had opened, Mrs. Freed beckoned her.

"Please, come in. I wish to speak with you."

Myrna hesitated, remembering her last private interrogation by a Freed, and bearing that same introduction, but did as bid, closing the door behind her. Dalton's mother motioned to a nearby chair, and Myrna nervously took a seat.

"Did you find your sister? Gladys only just told me she went missing."

"Yes, we found her in a room upstairs."

"I'm sure you must be relieved." At Myrna's nod, she continued, "So why don't you tell me what still has you upset?"

The woman's calm manner invited confidence, and Myrna briefly explained the situation.

"I had thought to take dinner with Sisi and try to ease her fears," she concluded. "Though I have no idea how to go about it, as I am now not without my own fears to travel by train."

"It was such a horrible ordeal for a child to suffer, for anyone to suffer." Mrs. Freed sympathized and paused, as if considering her next words. "Your sister is such a calming influence. Such a quiet child."

Myrna wondered if they spoke of the same girl. Sisi was anything but quiet, though compared to the exuberant Rebecca, Myrna could understand why Mrs. Freed thought her calm.

"My granddaughter and your sister have bonded as if they are kindred spirits. Before you came, I hadn't once seen Rebecca smile, not since my son's accident." She glanced at the patterned rug. Myrna didn't feel it appropriate to intrude into her thoughts so waited and said nothing. "Your sister is good for Rebecca, as a stabilizing influence and as a friend."

Suspicious by the direction of the conversation, Myrna tightly clasped her hands where they rested in her lap. "I'm sorry for your loss and grateful to you for allowing us to stay at your manor to convalesce."

"You don't have to go."

"No, I do." Her voice came out strained.

"Given the circumstances, do you honestly feel that your sister has had a chance to fully recover from that night? For that matter, have you? Do you not think it too soon to travel?"

"Exactly what are you saying?" Myrna asked carefully.

Mrs. Freed rose from the piano bench, taking the chair across from Myrna. "I've given the matter a great deal of thought. I've watched how you interact with your sister. She tells me you taught her to read?"

Myrna tried to follow, better yet to understand. "A lesson in progress."

"Then you do tutor Sisi?"

"In what manner I can." Myrna's heart rate increased.

"You seem like a respectable young woman, well learned in such skills and no stranger to social decorum."

"I'm sorry." Myrna shook her head. "I don't understand."

"Rebecca has long been in need of a governess. I wish to offer you the position—"

"No—I can't!" Myrna practically jumped to her feet, wishing to flee but managed to compose herself. "Forgive me, but I cannot accept your offer."

Mrs. Freed looked at her in clear surprise. "Sisi would receive every advantage that Rebecca does, studying alongside her. I assure you, she'll want for nothing and have her needs met. Both of you will. You may keep your present rooms, and the pay would be generous."

"You are very kind, Mrs. Freed, but we don't belong here."

"Nonsense. You are most welcome to stay."

Myrna doubted Dalton would feel the same consideration.

"May I ask, Miss McBride, are there other obligations which would prevent you from accepting my offer?"

Myrna winced at the appropriate form of address, twisting her mother's wedding ring on her finger. "How can you offer me the position, knowing so little about me and... and knowing what you do know?"

Mrs. Freed glanced at the ring. Myrna's face grew uncomfortably hot, and she moved her hand out of view, in the folds of her skirt, certain the questions would now follow. But the woman only smiled.

"I have not failed to note your qualities. With Sisi, you are gentle but not lacking in authority. Kind. Compassionate. It's clear she adores you. Perhaps I should not admit this, but Rebecca can be somewhat...unruly. She's been spoiled dreadfully and needs a guiding hand. A governess, with the qualities you possess."

"But I've never been a governess. I've only taken care of my sister."

"And you've done a remarkable job. Should you agree to the position, you'll not regret it." Her smile grew mysterious. "Indeed, the timing of events works well for all those involved."

"The timing?"

"You and Sisi will have a home, all that you need, a place to heal. Rebecca will have a companion her age and a governess. And I will have the delight of hearing children's laughter again, so long missing from this gloomy house—the laughter I've heard all week. I see God's handiwork involved here."

Myrna averted her eyes, uneasy with the subject of divine intervention. Where had God been when her family suffered from a scandal of half-truths and were forced to move? Where had God been when Papa died, handicapped, with a broken heart, after the loss of a wife who had worked herself into an early grave?

"At least consider taking the position for a short time," Mrs. Freed urged. "If you're not happy here come spring, you could leave."

A shaft of light brightened the room. Startled, Myrna looked in that direction.

The master of the manor stood on the threshold, his bearing formidable, his very presence enough to stop her heart and capture her breath.

"May I have the night to think about it?" Myrna whispered to Mrs. Freed.

"Of course. You may give me your answer in the morning."

"I must return to Sisi. You'll excuse me?"

"Yes, dear. Have a restful night. Should you agree to my offer, we will discuss the details tomorrow. It is my hope that there will be many other dinners we might share."

Myrna quickly sidestepped Dalton, not daring to look at him after that last remark.

Mrs. Freed might anticipate her presence, but she felt certain her taciturn son would not share his mother's enthusiasm, and she had no desire to linger and find out.

Running across one of the maids, she passed along her request of a dinner tray then took the stairs to join her sister.

Once she entered the spacious bedchamber that their entire old tenement could have fit into, leaving half the room to spare, she found Sisi curled up and lying on her side on the canopy bed. She clutched a china doll to her heart. Her eyes were closed, her breathing steady.

"Oh, Sisi, whatever shall I do?" she whispered, not wishing to wake her. She sat on the edge of the mattress and smoothed the child's tangle of curls.

Myrna wanted the best for her little sister, always, and had striven to achieve that. But one disappointment after another had been the scope of Sisi's young life. In one week, Myrna had seen an astounding transformation—Sisi happy, lively, excited to have a friend. Everything Mrs. Freed offered seemed like a dream too spectacular to believe credible. Only one shadow lingered to mar its sunny landscape....

The master of Eagle's Landing.

Her misgivings that spanned years warred with the desire to accept such a fortuitous proposal, and Myrna struggled to put aside selfish qualms and concentrate on doing what was best for her sister. The longer she considered the prospect, the clearer became the choice to be made.

May God help her.

If truly He did care.

"Please tell me I did not come upon what I fear to have just heard."

"Dalton, do come inside and cease from lurking in the doorway like a grumpy bear. Come now, stop your scowling."

Letting out a frustrated breath through his teeth, he closed the door and approached.

"Mother, you do realize that by putting me in the position of managing the estate, I should have a say in how it's run when it comes to the employment of those chosen?"

"Of course, dear. Shall I ring for some tea?"

"No, thank you. Please tell me you haven't hired Miss McBride as a replacement for Gladys?"

"Heavens, no."

"Well, that's a relief."

"She's to be Rebecca's new governess."

*"What?"* He sank to the chair Myrna had just vacated. "You're not serious?"

"I am. She's intelligent and well educated, a good guardian to her sister..."

"She has deceived me from the start and still wears a ring to display the lie."

"Did she actually tell you she was married? Or did

you rush to assumptions as has been your habit since you were a boy?"

Her rebuke came gentle but still flayed his pride. "Mother, the fact is *she is* still wearing that ring. We know nothing about the woman or where she comes from."

"And yet, you brought her here."

He was strongly beginning to regret such a rash decision.

"What else was I to do? Leave her and her little sister to freeze to death? But I had no intention of them securing a permanent place in this household, and especially not having that woman become a governess to my niece!"

She lifted her chin. "She is my granddaughter, let's not forget. Or do you suddenly question my love for Rebecca and ability to make sound decisions with regard to her? I've done so since her mother died, I'll remind you. I still run this household. I'm not yet in my dotage."

He pushed a tense hand through his hair. "Yes, yes, but your heart is too kind. You tend only to see the good in people, ignoring their blatant flaws."

"And you, my dear, do exactly the opposite. Every young woman is not Giselle."

Disturbed that she would introduce such a sensitive topic, his eyes snapped to hers. Her features were kind, but he looked away, unable to accept her sympathy.

"Miss McBride hardly seems the type to be a governess," he insisted quietly.

"She might surprise you. She seems a woman of many hidden talents."

He huffed out a laugh devoid of amusement. Myrna McBride had definitely surprised him on more than one occasion since meeting her a week ago. His mother was right—Myrna was certainly not what she appeared.

"Perhaps she might even make sense of your brother's notes."

"That won't happen." He would never give her the opportunity. Recognizing the grief in her quiet words, he calmed. "I won't let you down, Mother. I won't let all of what Grandfather built be lost."

She reached out and took his hand. "Dalton, you've never given me a moment's regret. You're very strong to bear such burdens. Your life has been riddled with them, ever since you were a boy…." Her voice cracked. Troubled, he cast his eyes to their clasped hands. "And now you've been given a full plate as a young man of twenty-two. I wish you never had to suffer. Only through reliance on the Lord will you overcome the obstacles and rise above the storm. I made that truth my fortress, the one gift of any true meaning I've passed down to my children."

He knew the verse well. It had become the household creed when his great-grandparents were alive.

"The strength of eagles, Dalton. That we may soar and not fall."

He nodded to show he understood, though he still struggled with faith in that area.

"Try to be more lenient of Miss McBride. Continue to rely on the charity that I know resides in your heart, that first saved a young woman in need, and be the honorable man I raised you to be." She patted his hand before releasing it.

He shook his head at her determined naïveté.

"So we are to close a blind eye to her continued deceit and pray she doesn't steal the family silver then run off into the night?" He spoke, only half in jest.

"Silver is only metal, a commodity that can be replaced. A person's soul cannot."

He chuckled dryly, having expected such an answer. "Sometimes your arguments defy all worldly logic. Yet deep down, they strike a bizarre chord of reason."

Her smile was cunning. "The wisdom that comes with

the experience of years, my boy. I cannot pretend to understand why Miss McBride felt such a pretense necessary, but I sense she's unhappy. I think she needs us as much as we need her."

"And there, once again, you have lost me."

His mother laughed. "Give it time, Dalton, and you'll see. If she agrees, it will be for a trial period, until the spring."

Dalton awaited the melting snows and the blooming flowers with an eagerness he had never before anticipated.

Myrna justified her decision to stay at Eagle's Landing—a place that was good for her sister, and which paid her a handsome wage that helped replenish all her family had lost—with a resolve to steer clear of her new master whenever possible. Thankfully, he seemed just as determined not to cross paths with her, his sudden appearance followed by a hasty exit from the doorway of whatever room she inhabited a clear sign of his similar disinterest. Breakfasts and luncheons were taken in the morning room with the girls. Dinners were shared in the great dining hall with the family and Dalton presiding at the head of the long table in brooding silence.

Soon, however, she reasoned that fate must have a wicked sense of humor. No matter their mutual disregard for one another's company, in that first week, in a house so enormous, Myrna crossed paths with the man what must be a half-dozen times a day.

The second week proved no better.

Nor did the third.

"Miss McBride," Rebecca interrupted Myrna's cynical train of thought. "Since the snows have mostly melted and it's not so cold as it was, after lessons can we go outside for a walk?"

"May we, and it's still cold."

"But not as cold as it was," Rebecca insisted.

Myrna had quickly learned that the wee mistress of the manor had a will as strong as the walls of stone that made up the fortress. In most matters where the situation warranted the need, Myrna remained firm, but she could see no true reason to deny the girl's hopeful request. After what seemed an eternal winter, it would be nice to escape the stifling mansion, along with a more than probable glimpse of its disturbing owner.

"Very well, Rebecca. If you and Sisi bundle up warmly, I suppose—"

"Yay!" Rebecca jumped up and clapped her hands.

Sisi's smile was bright. "May we look for the eagle's nest Mrs. Freed spoke of?"

"This time of year, they would not have returned—"

"Oh, and you must see the pretty place by the water." Rebecca had turned back to Sisi. "Mama used to take me there. The ducks go there. And bluebirds, too."

"I doubt the bluebirds or ducks would be there yet," Myrna tried again and failed. The girls chattered excitedly, and she could tell that any further hope for teaching the difference between a noun and an adjective would be lost in the anticipation of the hunt for nonexistent birds.

She closed the book. "That's enough for today. Go get your coats and scarves and…"

The words were barely out of her mouth when the girls jumped up from their chairs with eager squeals of delight and made an excited beeline for the door.

"Hats," she finished, shaking her head in wry amusement. She went to her room to don her own outerwear.

Once outside, the air wasn't as cold as previous days, but they could see their breath in puffs of white vapor. Myrna looked with concern toward her little sister, who seemed fine. The constant nurturing with hot toddies and warmed bricks at their feet had been an aid to them both, and on occasion Myrna felt petty to be so suspicious of the Freeds' generosity.

Neither could she shake what former experience had taught her.

The girls walked ahead in the snow, their eyes turned up to the cloudy sky, likely in search of absent bluebirds. In their coats and matching winter hats, they stood out against the bleak canvas of winter; Rebecca with her dark sausage-roll curls spilling from her velvet crimson cap and Sisi with brown hair just as springy falling over a soft wool coat of peacock blue. The two walked hand in hand, a bounce to their steps, and Myrna was glad she had sacrificed the sting of pride to accept the gift of Rebecca's castoff clothing for her little sister. To return to town and try to locate Sisi's coat from the wreckage had seemed a foolish endeavor.

The girls stopped suddenly on the path. Rebecca whispered in Sisi's ear, and they both turned their heads to stare at Myrna.

"Is there a problem, girls?"

"Uncle Dalton is visiting Papa's grave. Can we—*may we*—go see him?"

Myrna's breath caught. She looked past the girls to the evergreens that towered ahead like rows of flocked sentinels in pristine white. To the right, a scattered patch of headstones revealed the family's losses, and Myrna's heart lurched when she caught sight of Dalton's tall form. With his back to them and head bowed he remained unaware of their presence. She watched him slowly drop to one knee in respect and put his hand out to sweep snow from a stone. The vulnerable and rare sight of the formidable master of the estate appearing lost and somewhat forlorn brought a film of moisture to cloud her vision. She blinked the tears from her eyes.

"Not today." She took both girls' gloved hands and led

them back to the house. "Your uncle doesn't need to be disturbed."

Sisi looked up at her. "Don't you like Uncle Dalton, Myrna?"

She winced at the familiarity. "Mr. Freed to you, and why should you ask such a thing?"

"Because you always run from him."

The reply irritated her. "I don't run from him—"

"But Uncle Dalton runs from Miss Myrna, too," Rebecca corrected.

In frustration, Myrna hurried their steps along the path. "What complete and utter nonsense. Neither of us *runs* from the other."

"Whenever Uncle Dalton comes into the room, he goes away if you're there."

"And when you see him in the corridor, you go away," Sisi added.

"We have nothing to talk about." Despite the cold, Myrna's face burned with heat.

"But you have lots to talk about with Mrs. Freed," Sisi insisted.

"Sisi, that's enough."

"Don't you like Uncle Dalton?" Rebecca insisted.

"I was hired to be your governess. Not to be your uncle's companion. Now let us speak no more of this."

"But you're not Nana's companion, either, and you talk to her—"

"Children must learn to mind those older and wiser, and that includes you, young miss."

Thankfully, that put an end to their interrogation, but Myrna didn't fail to notice the covert look that passed between the girls. Hopeful that she had imagined any impending mischief, Myrna hurried her charges toward the back entrance.

# Chapter 6

Dalton straightened from his hunched position and stood to his feet. A short thaw days ago had allowed the ground to be broken so as to bury his brother's body.

"I let you down, Roger, and for that, I'm sorry. I should have somehow made you listen. But I vow to be the uncle Rebecca needs and fill the gap in your absence."

He whisked away the dampness wetting his lashes. Inadvertently his eyes flicked to another grave marker, behind his brother's. Drawn to it, he stood in solemn remembrance before the cold granite stone.

Roger was not the only one he had failed.

Leaning down he brushed snow from the engraved angel and traced a wing with his gloved fingertip. "Sweet Alyssa…"

Emotion clutched his throat a second time, and hurriedly he rose, taking a step in retreat.

It had taken him years to shun the past and move forward. Giselle's deceit of seven months ago had taken him unaware and sidetracked him momentarily. But now he must mend the broken pieces and become to his family what they needed, the sole reason he'd come home.

In the distance, he noticed three figures just as they turned the corner of the house. The girls and, from the fiery shine of auburn hair beneath the hat, the new governess. From the quick pace she set, hurrying the children along, he felt certain they had spotted him.

Dalton wasn't the only one to evade contact in the three weeks since Myrna McBride had taken the post, their attempts at avoidance sometimes dryly amusing, often bordering on the absurd. Planning his schedule to avert situations where they might be inclined to come in contact hadn't helped. They still managed to run across each other's paths habitually when he left the sunny library he'd made into his office.

Myrna had been in their home a month now and given them no cause to regret hiring her, but Dalton still lingered on the rigid side of caution, never forgetting that she once practiced deceit. To this day she wore her mother's ring, the ploy foolish since no one in the household remained ignorant to her ruse. No matter her faults, his mother's rebuke with regard to Dalton's churlish behavior had found its mark, and he struggled not to judge the new governess but instead give her the benefit of the doubt and practice tolerance—and kindness.

Once the dinner hour approached, Dalton found that resolve put to the test upon entering the parlor and finding her there alone. She looked beyond him as if expecting the others.

"The girls aren't with you?"

"No. Should they be?"

"Rebecca mentioned that she was going to speak with you, and Sisi was with her. They must be with your mother. She came by the playroom earlier."

"They never came to the library, though I stepped out for a moment and could have missed them."

"I see. Well, then. I imagine they're with your mother and will walk through the door at any moment."

According to the mantel clock, five minutes ticked by as they waited for the customary dinner summons and the rest of their party. The new maid popped into the parlor and gave a nervous curtsy.

"Beggin' your pardon, Mr. Freed, but I was told to tell you dinner is served."

"Thank you…Daisy, is that right?"

She blushed and smiled shyly. "Yes, sir."

"We'll be there shortly, Daisy."

He turned to Myrna once the maid left. The governess looked at him as if he had shed his skin. "Is there a problem?"

"How many servants do you employ that you find yourself uncertain of their names?"

He chuckled at her awestruck question, couldn't help himself.

"Forgive me. I didn't mean to be rude. Daisy took the spot of a maid who left our service recently. Gladys." He approached and held out his arm. "Mother probably went directly to the dining room with the children and forgot to tell us. Shall we?"

She looked at the sleeve of his waistcoat before finally taking his arm. They walked through the dim corridor and toward the dining hall.

"As to your question, we employ nine servants, yourself included. The cook and her assistant, who is her daughter, the main housekeeper, Miss Browning, who is in charge of the upstairs and downstairs maids, of which there are three, the driver, the groundskeeper, who is also the cook's husband, and soon I may have to hire an accountant—or perhaps a linguist, if I cannot translate the books." He spoke half in jest.

They reached the dining hall and moved through the entrance, both coming to a stop at the sight of the long table bearing only two place settings. Dalton's, at the head, the second one next to it and closer than Myrna usually sat. A candelabra glowed warmly near that. The cook's daughter, a brunette with frizzed curls, entered the room from another entrance, carrying the first course.

"Nora, has my mother taken ill? Where are the children?"

"The mistress said she was feeling a bit under the weather and wished to dine upstairs with the girls for a change."

"Are the girls all right?" Myrna asked in alarm.

"Yes, miss. She mentioned how she never spends time with her granddaughter lately and wanted to."

"I should go and collect Sisi."

"Oh, no, miss," the maid blurted before Myrna could fully turn away. "Her instructions were explicit. You're to take the evening off and enjoy a meal without worrying over your duties."

Dalton shook his head in disbelief, wondering what his mother could be thinking and strongly suspecting her motives.

Nora bustled to the table with a silver tureen and ladled soup into two bowls. While she worked, Dalton exchanged glances with Myrna, who looked both bemused and addled.

"I think we've been hoodwinked."

"I think you're right."

It was ironic that for weeks Dalton had done all within his power to avoid her presence, and now, thanks to his mother's evident maneuvering, Myrna was to be his sole dinner companion.

He studied her a moment, undecided. She made no excuse to quit the room, so he extended his hand toward the table. "Shall we?"

A slight nod was his answer. He held her chair out for her to be seated. Her eyes flicked to him, wary, but she took a seat.

Good grief. Did she think that he would pull the chair away from her like some uncouth cad? True, they had not always been on the best of speaking terms when they did speak, but he wasn't a fiend, which, by her anxious expression, was exactly what she thought him.

After offering the blessing, he noted her tense actions as she slipped her spoon into the spiced broth. She did not eat, only moved the utensil around the bowl.

Dalton inwardly sighed. This would get them nowhere quickly, and he did not wish her to starve.

"We got off on a bad footing." He introduced the topic they had avoided for weeks. "If you are agreeable, perhaps we can put that day behind us and begin anew?"

"You're no longer fearful that I might abscond with the family silver?"

Determined to be civil, he quenched his immediate suspicion that she had eavesdropped on that conversation with his mother.

"If you should try, your tracks would stand out in the snow," he answered just as dryly and watched her lift her surprised gaze from her plate and to his eyes. "Not to mention the dreadful clatter that lugging around a bag of silver would cause—which would surely give your location away."

A wash of pink colored her skin at his light teasing. He smiled in amusement, grateful when she did likewise. His brand of humor wasn't always understood or appreciated, but at least in this instance it helped to ease the atmosphere considerably. She relaxed and began to eat, opening the conversation with her adventures in being a governess.

"So how is my niece faring?" Dalton asked as Daisy brought the second course.

He watched Myrna cut her roast chicken into the smallest morsels he'd ever seen. "She's doing well." She slipped a fragment in her mouth, barely chewing.

"Come now, it's clear you're holding something back. I know she can be a little hellion at times."

"She is rather…lively."

He laughed at that. "A kind name for her rambunctious proclivities. And her studies?"

"In matters of reading comprehension and art, she excels. Her handwriting, however, is atrocious."

"Obviously an inherited trait," he said dryly, thinking of his brother.

"It's nothing I haven't dealt with before."

"Sisi?"

"No, she's still learning to print her letters. My father…" She fidgeted and set down her fork. "He had an accident before Sisi was born and never fully recovered the full use of his hand but insisted on writing his own correspondence. One winter, he lost his voice and needed to communicate through handwriting. I took care of him then, and after he died, I found letters he'd written." She blotted her mouth with a napkin. "Forgive me. I didn't mean to go on so."

"I'm sorry for your loss." He spoke gently, seeing she was upset.

Her eyes held a distressed shine as she looked at him. "You also suffered a loss, a recent one, with your brother."

"Yes, it's what brought me back home."

"I never said so, but I'm sorry to hear it."

A slow grin edged his lips.

Aware of the words she used, her eyes widened. "Oh, dear. I'm sorry…for your loss. I didn't mean that the way it sounded."

"But on occasion you *have* felt that way?" His smile remained intact.

"Do you wish me to lie, Mr. Freed? Or to speak the truth?"

"Truth is always the wisest choice, Miss McBride, but in this case it need not be stated."

She let out a soft laugh, a pleasure to hear.

The remainder of the meal passed in a camaraderie of ease that Dalton would never have believed possible an hour before. Indeed, at any time these past four weeks. They spoke of everything—from weighty matters of life and death to more trivial generalities. Whatever the topic, her insightful answers astounded him. Had it not been too cold, he might have suggested a stroll in the garden, finding himself unexpectedly reluctant to leave her company.

"Thank you," she said while he held her chair for her as she rose from the table.

With the emotions of the moment governing his actions, Dalton fell into step beside her once they left the dining room. If she was surprised by his continued company, she gave no indication.

They continued the mundane discussion of his boyhood, questions he did not care to answer, much less dwell on, and soon he turned the conversation back to her.

"You are accomplished in many areas," he said as they came abreast of the music room and stopped. "Do you play, perchance?"

She glanced into the dim chamber at the piano. "I never had the opportunity for lessons. My mother did, though. Do you play?"

"Up until my fourteenth year."

At her clear amazement to receive an affirmative answer, he grinned. "Something Mother insisted on for all her children, stating the practice good to hone concentration and dexterity."

"And did it work?"

"Some days, I have cause to wonder." He shook his head wryly.

"Perhaps I should ask if you might play for me."

"I wouldn't wish to cause undue suffering. I've not laid my fingers to the ivory for years."

"Never mind. I wasn't serious. I should check on Sisi. Good night, Mr. Freed."

"That's not the way to the main staircase," he said once she walked away.

She stopped and glanced back at him. "I left a book in the parlor and want to return it to the library."

"One of the maids can tend to it."

"So can I."

He covered the short distance. "That's what the maids are for."

"I'm not accustomed to servants waiting on me, especially when I can easily perform the task just as well."

She continued down the hall. Again, he fell in step beside her.

"I've taken such privileges for granted my entire life. I had no wish to offend."

"I wasn't offended. Despite what you might think, I don't offend easily."

Inside the parlor, she plucked up a book from a chair cushion and held it up. "Here it is."

At the nervous little hitch in her voice, Dalton again endeavored to put her at ease. As they strolled to the library, passing the music room a second time, he reintroduced a former topic.

"You mentioned that your mother played the piano?"

"Yes. I never heard her, though. I wasn't allowed."

"Not allowed?"

At her puzzling words, he glanced at her. For a moment she did not speak.

"When Father had the accident, Mother sought employment. Father was a stonecutter."

"A mason?"

"No, he worked with gemstones. Cut them and set them."

"A jeweler?"

"Yes."

They approached the library, and he opened the door for her. The fire that earlier blazed with life now gently flickered in low flames.

"I don't recall that being here," she wondered aloud, looking toward the desk.

"I had it brought in. I find my brother's study intolerably dark and oppressive. The windows of this room give off plenty of light for me to work."

"Oh." She seemed at a sudden loss for words.

"Please, sit down."

"I should go."

"It's early yet. I'd like to hear more about your parents. Your father, did he have his own shop?"

"Yes, but he broke his wrist." She hesitated then set the book down on the entrance table. Warily she approached the hearth and took a seat. He took the chair opposite. "The bone never set right." She shook her head sadly. "He tried to find other work, but…"

"Was your mother a piano teacher, then?"

"No. She became a companion to a reclusive dowager and would play for her." As always, each of her words seemed carefully measured before she spoke them, as if fearful to say too much. "We lived in the carriage house. Father was the dowager's driver, though she rarely left the estate."

"She chose a married woman with a family for her companion?"

"The dowager knew Mother's family well." Again Myrna hesitated. "Mother was the daughter of a respected attorney who fell into dire straits. I never knew the particulars. I was too young to understand and they never spoke of it in my presence, but I gather there were bad feelings between my grandparents and my mother. I never met them. As far as I know, before their deaths, they never contacted her."

"You are sure they're deceased?"

She gave a terse nod, her eyes going to the fire. "Then, almost two years ago, I discovered I had a cousin, through a letter Papa left me. He—he also contacted my family through a letter. I was never told anything before Papa died, never knew he even had a brother." Her manner grew distant. "It was just the four of us. Sisi, myself, my parents. No one else…"

Stunned, he watched a change come over her. Misery clouded her features and her eyes brimmed with tears she tried to hide, turning her face to the hearth.

With no intent but to extend kindness, he offered her his handkerchief. She hesitated then took the silk with a muffled thank-you. She dabbed at her eyes and nose and held it crumpled to her mouth, her hand shaking.

"I apologize, sir. I don't know what came over me." She stood awkwardly to her feet and swayed. In reaching for the chair arm, she dropped his handkerchief and missed the chair, as well.

He grasped her shoulders to steady her.

"Easy. Sit down before you fall."

"I'm fine. I only stood too quickly."

"The doctor said that you could have episodes and to be cautious."

"That was weeks ago," she argued but did as directed.

Dalton knelt before her. She glanced at him in guarded shock. He retrieved the scrap of silk from the rug, but she didn't take it this time. A tear trembled at the edge of her jaw and he touched the cloth to it.

"I really don't know what came over me," she whispered, her glistening eyes never leaving his.

"Have you once taken the time to grieve?" he asked, brushing at the track the tear left behind.

"I…" She frowned, then stopped whatever she was about to say. "There wasn't time for such things. Sisi is my priority. I must put her first."

"Take it." He pressed his handkerchief into her hand. "I have an ample supply."

The hint of a smile ghosted her lips. "At home, I would have had to pay half a week's wages to acquire such an extravagance." A frown creased her brow, as if she thought of what she had no wish to remember. He disliked seeing her upset and wondered about her previous circumstances that she would consider a scrap of silk a luxury.

"I may take much for granted, having never been in material want, but that doesn't mean I haven't suffered or don't understand loss. I care that you're in pain."

"It's nothing." Her damp lashes swept downward, provoking another tear.

"I beg to differ."

His finger and thumb touched her chin, gently tilting it upward. His goal was realized when her startled eyes met his. Eyes the color of evergreen shimmered with moisture, the dying firelight casting her face in a rosy-orange glow, her hair illuminated in deep red as if the flames themselves glowed within. Her lower lip trembled as he stared, and he dropped his gaze to her mouth, the urge to discover if it was as soft as it appeared overwhelming him.

Slowly, he leaned into her. She remained as fixed as stone. With tenderness he brushed his lips against hers, finding them as soft as satin, and felt the sudden exhalation of her warm breath and the give of her lips as she reciprocated the act.

The pleasurable contact lasted no more than seconds before he felt her tense. He broke their kiss.

"Why did you do that?" she whispered, her voice trembling with distress.

Clearly she no longer welcomed his spontaneous advance, and Dalton decided it wise not to argue that she had kissed him back. "I apologize." He dropped his fingers from her chin and straightened from his kneeling position, moving to stand before the fire. "I don't know what came over me." That much was true.

What in blazes had possessed him to kiss her?

"I fear we have reached another misunderstanding." Her voice came determined, with a hint of betraying nervousness. "I'm not the kind of woman to have a—a dalliance with my employer, with any man."

Good grief. Did she think he would now try to bed her? "Calm yourself, Miss McBride. It was no more than a kiss. It meant nothing. You were upset. I wished to offer comfort."

"I should go."

He gave a stiff nod. "Yes, you should."

Still he would not look at her, his concentration on the flames. He only knew she left by the click of the door.

Dalton's eyes fell closed at the severe finality of such a quiet sound and the strange hollow feeling it left within the region of his chest.

Myrna hurried to her room instead of Sisi's, not wishing for her sister to see her in such a state of distraught confusion. Her countenance in the looking glass stunned her—eyes overbright, cheeks flushed, expression soft—and she turned her back on the disquieting image.

Words from long ago haunted her soul.

"Myrna," her mother had said, "you're eleven now and old enough to understand. You may hear…troubling things about your sister. About me."

"What things, Mama?"

"Lies, Myrna. All lies. Your father and you two girls are all that's important. You three are my reason for doing what I must in order that we survive. And sometimes, darling, sacrifices must be made." Her eyes had been pained as she hugged Myrna close.

Myrna had no idea what *things* or *sacrifices* Mother spoke of. But as the year progressed, she noticed disturbing changes in her parents' behavior. Her father grew sullen and distant, her mother almost desperate to please him. At times, when they thought her asleep, she would hear their low, heated voices, often arguing about one man, the wealthy dowager's son who'd come to live at his mother's estate the year before Sisi was born. Strangers would comment on Sisi being a replica of their mother but not having one trait that belonged to Father. Myrna thought nothing of it until the day that changed her concept of the world forever.

Her mother forbade her to visit the mansion, but one morning she defied the rule, curiosity to see the home that loomed like a grand castle overriding the obedience she usually practiced. Mother had not seen her, but Myrna peeked through a parlor window and had seen her mother, near tears and standing in the arms of a well-dressed man, younger than Father—before her mother then pushed him away. The man grabbed her roughly, pulling her back and into his kiss. Her mother gave no struggle.

Myrna did not linger to see more and ran all the way home to the carriage house, horrified and confused.

As she grew older, she put together what she'd seen with snippets of gossip overheard and the manner in which people would look at Sisi. Despite her mother's earlier protestations, she recognized the truth. When Myrna was fourteen, her father woke her and told her they were leaving. Her mother was quiet but submissive, and the four of them escaped the estate in the night, eventually finding a dingy apartment in another city in their struggle to leave the past and its scandal behind. Myrna never doubted her mother's love for them, but it had been difficult to forgive her faults, even if Mother *had* been bullied into betraying her vows, as it seemed. Yet scandal had a manner of catching up to the unwary, and not until Myrna confronted her own dark horror, related to those days when they lived in the carriage house, did she truly understand being a victim.

She shook her head, hoping to free her mind from its shackles to the past.

*Why did he kiss her?*

Had he never done so, she would not now be reliving those awful days of her childhood. In frustration, she sat on the edge of the made bed and grabbed a pillow to her chest.

She had begun to hope Dalton was different, that she had been hasty in her snap judgment of his character.

*It was no more than a kiss. It meant nothing....*

His hurtful words mocked her, and she pushed away that one moment of weakness when the startling liberty he'd taken *did* mean something to her. By his words, he proved he was no better than the dowager's son or her tormentor of last year.

He was certainly no Mr. Rochester, though her current employer did share some of his less than flattering traits—often distant, brooding, steeped in mystery. And she was *not* Jane Eyre, even if she also came from impoverished means and had obtained the position of governess to his young ward in a vast manor that also seemed full of dark secrets.

She stared at the book she had yet to return to Rebecca.

Often she found herself thumbing through its pages, re-reading various chapters. Why, she didn't know. Perhaps as a cautionary lesson to herself, since their situations were so eerily similar....

Though to fall in love with the master of the manor—that she *would never* do!

He had been charming and companionable at dinner, even if their recent discussion brought back harsh memories. Yet to him she was no more than a potential dalliance. His uninvited kiss and the words that followed proved he was a scoundrel.

Didn't they?

Determined not to give another thought to the exasperating man who presided over Eagle's Landing, Myrna tossed the pillow to the bed with more force than necessary, composed herself, then quit the room to check on her sister.

## Chapter 7

Today had been a good day, despite the cold, dreary rain.

Long, seemingly never-ending weeks had melted into the beginning of spring since the night Myrna shared dinner with Dalton. She separated the good days—when she had little to no contact with him and life progressed normally—from the bad ones, where the world seemed tilted on its axis and everything went wrong from the moment she stepped out of bed, including the return of their chance meetings. As a rule, she saw Dalton only in the evenings, at dinner, when he rarely spoke to her or acknowledged her existence. Their haphazard encounters in corridors and otherwise empty rooms came much less frequently in the past week, so it was with a shock that Myrna opened the door to the library that evening and found the master inside.

He looked up from his ledger in surprise.

"Oh! Pardon me, I was told you were in town. I'll return later."

Before she could make a hasty slip out the door, he stood to his feet.

"You've come to collect a book?"

She gave a short nod. "Yes, and to return one."

"By all means then, don't let me stop you."

"If you're sure it's no bother."

"I won't even notice you there."

His low words smarted though she didn't think his slight intentional. Not this time, at least. He sat back down and intently focused on his ledger as if it contained the president's final address to the nation.

Myrna made quick work of replacing a book of poetry to its proper place on the shelf, deciding to return later. She was halfway to the door when he spoke.

"You didn't find what you were looking for?"

Uncertain if she should relay her quest, she looked at him. "I was hoping to find a story suitable for the girls."

His expression was inscrutable. "Last row at this end, second shelf from the bottom you'll find a small collection of children's books."

"Thank you." She hurried past the freestanding bookcases to the back of the room, musty with the earthy scent of old books, an aroma not unpleasant but welcoming. Yet now was not the time to linger. She located the small section, their covers faded and worn.

As she emerged from within the literary haven, his attention dropped to and remained on the three books she held.

"I see you found them."

"Were they yours?" Something about his somber attitude gave her pause.

"No." He returned to his ledger and she felt as if she'd been dismissed. She moved to go.

"Miss McBride...?"

Again she turned.

"I trust the girls are doing well in their studies?"

Confused, she looked at him. Had he forgotten that his mother brought up the subject at dinner last night, and Myrna had given a full recounting then? Or perhaps he truly did shun her existence and chose not to listen.

"Yes, they are doing well."

"And you…" His voice came more softly. "Have you fully recovered from the accident? When last we talked you were unwell."

*Do you mean before or after you kissed me and told me it meant nothing?*

The words came unbidden to her mind and she ignored their unwelcome intrusion. She lowered her attention to the scrollwork that edged his desk.

"Other than a smattering of pain behind my eyes now and then, I'm well."

"You suffer from headaches?"

"On rare occasions." She wished now that she hadn't brought them up. "When I read too long into the night. It's nothing."

"I'm pleased that you've found a worthy pursuit to occupy your time, but it's best not to overdo. Perhaps another visit from the doctor would be wise."

"No, really, I don't wish to put him out of his way."

"Medicine *is* his profession. Besides, Mother mentioned that he's coming to visit this week. You'll need to speak with her to learn when."

Seeing no end to the matter and feeling as if she'd been given an order, Myrna reluctantly conceded. "Very well. If that's what you wish."

"It is."

The underlying amusement in his tone had her lift her eyes to his. They sparkled with mirth, something she did not often see. His lips twisted at the corners, bringing out a slight cleft in his cheek, something she had seen before, certainly, but never really noticed.

"As your employer it's my place to see to your welfare, since you're a member of this household. Though I would hope that my wishes are not the sole medium to ensure that you maintain good health."

His words, gently teasing, and the intent look he gave made her forget to breathe. Coming to herself with a start, Myrna looked away.

"If there's nothing else, sir?"

"No, that will be all."

Once outside the library, Myrna took her first steady breath since she entered the room and with it, regained her reason.

Bother it all, she didn't like a fuss when she was the object of attention. Dalton Freed was stubborn and impossible. Yet wholly unpredictable. Tonight he had been kind. Human, even. Not a wolf with the aim to devour, though she had yet to forget his tender kiss and wondered if she ever would.

Unable to locate Mrs. Freed downstairs, she ascended the stairs to the second level. At the sight of a door ajar, she approached, halting at the sound of women's voices and the stiff bustle and shake of material.

"Not like that, Daisy, circular motions." Genevieve's words came clear to Myrna. "Ye want to be buffin' the metal to a gloss."

"It's such a grand house, but so sad. I feel as if ghosts might be living here." Another woman's voice trailed off to a nervous whisper. "Sometimes I hear crying late in the night."

"Like as not it's the mistress, or have you forgotten she lost a son?"

"No, it's a child who's crying."

"Poff. There are two wee girls livin' here, as well."

"I know what I heard, and it wasn't like anything living and breathing on this earth…"

Myrna drew her brows together in confusion at the bizarre statement.

"What of the master?"

"You think he's the child crying?" Genevieve teased.

"No, of course not. But he's right handsome, don't you think?"

"You best keep your eyes on your work, Daisy." Genevieve's tone came more harshly. "Mr. Freed isn't the type to set his cap for the likes of you."

Myrna put her hand to her heart that raced a little faster at the mention of his name.

"He was engaged, you know."

"The master?"

"No, the black stallion in the stables. Of course the master!"

"You needn't be so uppity. I didn't know, did I? So? What happened to her?"

"A scandal that set every tongue wagging, but we're not to talk of it. It's the sole reason he left, ye ken."

They lowered their voices. Also interested, Myrna leaned closer to hear.

"Oh, do tell," Daisy begged. "Did he marry her?"

"He most certainly did not. He up and left. Moved to Boston to attend college—that's where he was when the former master passed on and—oh!"

Myrna jumped back in shock when she realized, too late, that they were exiting the room. Genevieve regarded her with alarm. The other maid, a young brunette, looked just as apprehensive.

"We didn't know you was there, miss." Genevieve fumbled an excuse and tucked a stray ginger-colored curl into her white, lace-trimmed cap. "I'm just showing Daisy the ropes. She's new."

Daisy bobbed an awkward curtsy, pinching the corner of her black skirt.

"Yes, we've met." Myrna offered a smile just as awkward, feeling just as discombobulated, as well as highly embarrassed to be caught eavesdropping. "I was looking for Mrs. Freed."

"This time of day she should be going over the menu with the cook."

"Thank you, Genevieve. Have either of you seen the girls?"

"No, miss."

Daisy shook her head and both maids hurried past and down the corridor.

Myrna mulled over what she'd just heard, oddly dismayed to learn the master was indeed the pitiless cad she thought him, in breaking some poor woman's heart by spurning her love. His behavior a scandal, his misdeeds ignored as if they never occurred. It was a benefit of the wealthy to pretend all offenses out of existence and expect their wishes met. That his ill-mannered behavior should come as such a surprise warranted the true shock. Some hidden part of her had hoped she was wrong in her estimation, but clearly, Dalton fit to form.

An affluent man not to be trusted.

After another encouraging talk from his mother with regard to his management of the family legacy, Dalton left the parlor and ran across the path of Genevieve and the new maid. Both girls smiled, their faces flushed. The new girl gave a little bob of a curtsy as if he was royalty. He lifted his brows in mild surprise and smiled at her, unable to remember if he'd ever received such an acknowledgment.

Genevieve frowned at Daisy then, to Dalton's amusement, did likewise.

"Good afternoon, ladies." He inclined his head and made to walk past them.

"Beggin' your pardon, sir, but have you seen the girls?"

"Are they missing again?"

Daisy giggled and Genevieve shook her head. "Don't rightly know, but Miss McBride asked. She seems to have lost them."

In a manor with close to a hundred rooms, including the servants' quarters, he wasn't surprised. So many places existed where mischievous children could hide. He'd spent half his boyhood discovering all of them.

"I'm sure they'll turn up eventually."

He continued down the corridor toward the main entrance. At the stairwell, a flurry of movement caught his eye. He looked up toward the second level, frowning when he saw the shadow on the wall that disappeared toward the stairs leading to the third floor.

Swiftly he went in pursuit.

Not surprised to find the door to the third room ajar, he noticed it was no longer empty.

The governess stood in the midst of the old playroom, taking a slow perusal of the long-neglected toys. Some were no longer covered with dustcloths, a few of those lying on the ground, one near a rocking horse with peeling paint. Another had been cast aside from a tall dollhouse in the replica of Eagle's Landing.

Her attention rested on the miniature dwelling, which looked as if it had only recently been crafted and never once touched. He winced.

"What are you doing in here?"

He had not intended his voice to sound so abrasive, and she whirled to face him.

"Mr. Freed!" Guilt flashed in her eyes.

"This room is no longer used."

"Yes, but—is this not a playroom? The dollhouse—"

"No." He gave her no opportunity to finish. Nor did he satisfy her curiosity. "We keep the door locked."

"But it was open." Again she stared at the dollhouse. "I thought at first it might be one of Rebecca's play areas."

He moved past her and whipped the sheet from the floor, spreading it over the small, three-story structure. "And now you know otherwise." He forced himself not to look at the long window covered by heavy drapery.

"You treat me as if *I* uncovered the toys."

At her tone of offense he dryly observed her. "You expect me to believe the sheets flew off the toys by themselves? Next will you tell me the toys came to life?"

*"I didn't touch them!* They were like that when I came in here."

He paused to consider. She had no reason to lie, not about something so inconsequential. His niece must have visited the forbidden room. He certainly could not imagine one of the maids leaving dust covers on the floor and would confront Rebecca at the earliest opportunity.

"It seems I must again ask pardon, Miss McBride. Surely, though, you understand why it was easy for me to reach such a conclusion? Finding you here like this."

"I expect little else. After all, you decided I must be a thief and practically accused me to my face. You have a habit of jumping to conclusions where I'm concerned, Mr. Freed, and quite frankly I wish you would stop doing that."

At her candid, unruffled response he regarded her in surprise. No servant had ever responded to him with such cheek. Though, oddly enough, he never thought of the governess as a true servant. He could offer the rejoinder that she'd given him little reason to think otherwise in her practiced game of deceit but suddenly was weary of the round and round carousel of barely veiled insults and innuendo between them.

He nodded. "You're right, I should. Trust is a difficult thing for me to extend."

Her mouth parted slightly in astonishment at his answer and her shoulders relaxed. "I suppose in that regard we're alike. Trust comes extremely hard for me. It always has. I've learned to rely on instinct alone since I was a child."

"Is *that* why you can be so stubborn…?"

Her chin sailed up and she crossed her arms over her chest. "You're one to talk about being stubborn! I've met mules that are more cooperative—"

He laughed in genuine amusement, and she blinked as yet again she was taken aback by his response.

"You don't have much experience with being in service, do you?"

"No." She dropped her arms back to her sides. "But if it means I'll be talked down to or bullied, I won't take that from any man. No matter his position over me."

"An admirable quality."

"You think so?" She sounded thoroughly befuddled, as if expecting a different reply.

"Certainly. Pardon my random teasing, Miss McBride. Another fault of mine. Never change who you are, and never take incivility from anyone." He moved to the door and waited, making clear he would not leave until she did. "I imagine your charges are looking for you."

"Actually, I was looking for them." She followed him to the corridor. "That's what led me here."

He frowned at the lock as he closed the door, deciding his niece must have found a skeleton key.

"Once Rebecca realizes it's time for the meal, she'll appear," he assured as they moved down the stairs.

"She thinks the world of you."

"I'm all the father she has, even if I'm no more than a guardian uncle."

They reached the second landing, and he took the first

step down to the main floor. She continued along the corridor then stopped. Both glanced back at each other at the same time.

"I suppose I'll be seeing you at supper, then."

Her soft statement bordered on a question, and he shook his head.

"I have plans in town."

He thought of the upcoming social gathering at the mayor's house, knowing it mandatory that he make an appearance, especially since his mother wasn't attending. Important associates would be present, and it was time Dalton publicly made his place known as head of the estate and all that entailed.

"Oh, I see." Myrna's answer came faint. "Well, good night then."

Dalton paused to watch her hasty retreat, wondering why it was so difficult to go, before he forced himself to descend the stairs.

## Chapter 8

The quiet in the parlor was unsettling, a perfect accompaniment to gloomy thoughts.

"Is something troubling you, my dear?"

Myrna started at the sudden words coming from the other occupant of the room, fidgeted on her stiff chair, then set her teacup on its saucer.

"Mr. Freed says that I act little like a servant," she blurted what she'd been dwelling on for the past several minutes. Every night after supper, since she attained the position of governess, she took tea and sweets with Dalton's mother in the parlor. The matriarch preferred a light dessert there as opposed to the heavy one served at the table, and over the weeks, Myrna had grown comfortable enough in her presence to join her. Mrs. Freed never treated her as if she didn't belong, and Myrna had begun to open up to her. "But then, I suppose I don't know how a governess should act."

"*My son* said that to you?"

Betraying heat crept to Myrna's face. "Yes, well, I was where I shouldn't have been, and he was angry. I shouldn't have reacted in kind."

"Where should you not have been?" Mrs. Freed asked in puzzlement.

Myrna gave a guilty shrug. "The third floor. The playroom. I thought it was Rebecca's. There are so many rooms in this house…" She trailed off noting the strain that swept across her employer's face as she stared into the nearby hearth fire. "Mrs. Freed? Are you ill?"

"No. Forgive my son's ill manners. He went through a difficult time when my Alyssa died." A sad smile edged her lips and she glanced at Myrna. "My daughter."

"Oh." Myrna blinked in shock. "I didn't know you had one."

"She was quite suddenly taken from me. Alyssa was seven when she died."

*Sisi's age,* Myrna thought with a protective edge of unease, though she didn't really fear Mrs. Freed's intentions toward her sister. The woman had been considerate and generous. But she sensed the reminder of her daughter was one reason Dalton's mother had persuaded Myrna to stay.

Mrs. Freed nodded, as if reading her thoughts. "Your sister reminds me of Alyssa. Sweet and quiet. Always a follower, as Sisi is to Rebecca. Sometimes that isn't wise." She looked away and shook her head, as if in remembrance. "My family has had to deal with much tragedy and suffering through the years. I lost my husband and four of my children, two stillborn. It is only through those terrible struggles that I have learned the sole way to survive is to place faith in God. In that manner alone, I've become strong enough to overcome life's sorrows."

Myrna said nothing, not comprehending how suffering could bring trust.

"There is a Scripture passage that I live by: 'But they

that wait upon the Lord shall renew their strength; they shall mount up with wings as eagles; they shall run, and not be weary; and they shall walk, and not faint.'" Mrs. Freed smiled. "Ever since the first Freed ancestor found this land upon which to build, almost a century ago, that Scripture passage has been the motto for this household. Josiah Freed sighted an eagle roosting on a high crag beyond the trees, near the water, and reasoned that for such a stalwart bird to have made his resting place here, this land was the perfect place on which to build his home. Eagle's Landing. A sign of strength and fortitude to all who reside within."

Myrna listened with interest.

"Eagles are amazing creatures. Shortly after I married my husband and he brought me to this estate, he told me that it's reputed that when they age, eagles renew themselves by plucking out their feathers to grow new ones and damaging their beaks and talons. They lose the desire to eat and can no longer see well, but they rest, alone, bathing in sunlight, and they endure until the time that their bodily appendages grow back and they're reborn into strength. Whether legend or reality, the eagle's travail teaches that no matter the state of one's personal adversities, if any man endures until the end, he can, with God's help, emerge victorious."

Her wise words made Myrna envious to know such strength, but she'd been taught since childhood to rely on her own strength to get by, however limited it sometimes was. Despite her sad debacles of the past year, she knew no other way to survive and felt apprehensive to change.

Mrs. Freed reached over to lay her hand on Myrna's, regaining her attention.

"What God does for the eagles, He can do for you, my dear. You have only to put your trust in Him."

Trust. There was that deceptive word. A boulder in her

path that she often needed to skirt and from which she only wished to run.

"Yes, thank you," she murmured in feeble response. "If you'll excuse me, Mrs. Freed, I think I'd like to take a short stroll before the night grows too cold." She felt almost frantic to leave the confinement of the house and seek fresh air, the walls sometimes, as now, feeling as if they were closing in on her. With her charges in bed, she had nothing to keep her indoors.

"Of course, my dear. Do take caution and bundle up warmly. And don't stray too far from the house."

Myrna nodded in smiling acknowledgment before leaving the parlor, unable to take offense by the woman's propensity to coddle. How long had it been since someone cared about her welfare without selfish motives to prompt them? Even Mrs. Freed's periodic references to God and her gentle persuasions to put faith in Him no longer upset Myrna, now that she'd grown accustomed to hearing such words.

She had no idea why she felt so restless, though the revelation of the deceased Alyssa had been a shock, making Myrna think of Sisi and how she'd almost lost her.

Once she donned her cape and exited the house through the kitchen door, not comfortable with using the front one when not with Rebecca, she thought back to the discovery of the shrouded rooms and Dalton's grim reactions to those surroundings. Had he been older than his sister? Younger? Had she died before he was born?

The questions wove into the fabric of her mind, blending with all she knew about the man, which was still so little.

She walked along the narrow path. The hardwoods and firs stood as strong silhouettes of black shadow rising several stories above her head on either side, causing her to feel insignificant in comparison. She drew the brisk air into her lungs, thankful for the clarity it gave her to think, though the subject under consideration remained a mystery.

Dalton Freed was the most confusing man she'd ever met. Stubborn, condescending, at times cruel with his sarcasm, but the flip side of his nature bespoke gentleness and a frank concern she had witnessed in no man, not even her father. In past weeks she witnessed in Dalton admirable traits she had not wished to see. Worse, she could not stop thinking about him.

A chill drizzle began to fall. Realizing she had wandered farther than she intended, she lifted the hood of her cloak over her head and changed direction. The path could barely be seen but dully glowed lighter than her surroundings, the trees or clouds having blocked out the globe of the moon.

What addled her senses was the realization that she coveted the feelings of warmth and protection Dalton engendered, and that frightened her. Whereas before she kept an eye out for sight of him to *avoid* him, this past week she found herself hoping first *to see* that glimpse of him. His kiss, which she often relived, added to the novel feeling of pleasant warmth that trickled through her blood at the memory. A truth she had not once allowed herself to dwell on—but now broke free.

Hidden fire singed her face, welcome in its heat but not in the recollection it incurred, and she forced herself to think of dour facts.

Dalton was the antithesis of safety. His life—his very character—steeped in secrets and scandal, and she wanted nothing more of scandals!

Lost in thought, Myrna did not heed the thrumming of hoofbeats at once. She whirled around to see a lone rider headed straight for her. Horror kept her fixed, her heart seeming to leap to her throat before she possessed the presence of mind to dart out of the way. In her haste, she stumbled and fell to the damp soil, using her hands to save her fall. From her horizontal position on the ground, she watched in terror as a huge black stallion reared up on hind legs, almost unseating its rider, who somehow managed to get his beast under control and calmed.

Pushing herself up to sit, Myrna lifted her eyes to see Dalton hurry toward her.

"Are you hurt?" he bit out in concern.

Dazed, she shook her head and allowed him to help her up, relying fully on his strength, since her legs trembled badly from the near miss.

Once she was on her feet, his demeanor changed. Holding her by the upper arms, he gave her a firm shake. "What in blazes are you doing in the middle of the road in the pitch-black of night? In that dark cloak, I couldn't see you. *You could have been trampled to death!*"

Remorse and embarrassment caused her to swing loose from his grasp.

"I was taking a walk."

"In the rain? In the night?" He posed the questions in sheer disbelief as if she were daft. "Did you dream you were a thirsty bat?"

She frowned. "The path leads directly to the house. I couldn't get lost if I tried. It didn't start raining till now."

"I refuse to stand here in what could become a downpour and argue semantics with you. Come." He took hold of her arm, turning toward his horse.

"I can walk." She held back, though she didn't try to break free this time, but he forced her along as if thinking she might.

"I've never heard such folderol! It's cold and wet and dark. You'll ride back with me."

She was given no choice—a common theme with Dalton, she had found—as he lifted her to the saddle. It wasn't her first time on a horse, but under such circumstances she felt as if it might as well be, and sat awkwardly in place.

He swung up behind her and took the reins. Feeling engulfed by the sensation of warmth, to be so close to this overpowering man who had occupied her thoughts for weeks, Myrna grew light-headed. He slipped one strong arm around her middle, holding her to him to keep her on his mount, but the act had the opposite effect, causing her to feel suddenly weak inside. Sure she would fall, she clutched the horse's mane more tightly as they took off at a brisk pace.

With the bizarre turn of events, she reminded herself that he was not Rochester, she was not Jane, the ironic encounter with her employer almost running her down with his stallion notwithstanding. He had secrets. Not a mad wife, only a jilted fiancée. She was the governess to his charge, but that's where all similarities ended.

She most certainly *was not* falling under the spell of her employer! The harrowing events of the night were all that were responsible for her winded breathlessness and the erratic beating of her heart.

He brought his stallion to a halt before the entrance and helped Myrna to the ground without a word, the ease with which he did so emphasizing his strength. She felt relieved the accident of several weeks ago caused no more than brief and minor damage to his arm. Before she could form words of gratitude, he turned his horse and rode toward the stables, disappearing into the night.

Stunned and relieved by his swift and silent exit, she recollected her frayed wits and approached the steps, hoping the door was unlocked and she wouldn't have to ring the bell for someone to let her inside. She wanted no one to see her in such a state, her dress and cloak muddied from her fall, with thick tendrils of hair loosened and dangling from lost pins. Thankfully, nothing barred her entrance, but as Myrna approached the foyer, Miss Browning hurried toward her, taking the last stairs down.

"Miss McBride! Thank goodness. It's your sister. She's been calling for you."

Myrna rushed up the winding stairs. "Did something happen?" she asked the housekeeper who followed at her heels.

"I'm sorry. I don't know."

Myrna burst into Sisi's bedchamber. Her tiny sister sat in the middle of the bed, thankfully in one piece and well, save for the tears streaming down her cheeks. She clutched one of Rebecca's dolls to her chest.

"Myrna," she sobbed pitifully.

Heedless of her disheveled state, Myrna hurried forward and drew her into her arms. "What happened, my pet?"

"I dreamed I was on the train and couldn't get off and there was fire everywhere and I couldn't find you." She clutched Myrna hard. "I never want to leave here—please say we won't. Please, Myrna," she cried into her shoulder.

At a loss for words, Myrna held her. This wasn't the first night since the collision that Sisi had awakened from a nightmare. Her eye caught motion and she looked toward the open door.

Still wearing his long outer coat, traces of mud smearing the front from where he had held her against him, Dalton stood at the threshold and stared at her distraught sister. He lifted his eyes to Myrna. In them, she found tender compassion.

Her heart skipped an astonished beat before he offered a slight nod and walked on.

"Please, Myrna?" Sisi whimpered, begging for an answer.

She continued to look at the empty spot where Dalton had been, then hugged her sister closer, kissing her head of tousled curls. "Don't worry. I'll not let harm come to you, Sisi. Never again."

\* \* \*

Dalton transferred his brother's notes into a clean ledger. He frowned at the next line, his pen poised above parchment.

Amounts owed or accrued presented little problem. Numbers were easier to figure out than names. Whoever this entry was, according to the ledger, Dalton would need to visit wherever they were located to obtain information about profit. Apparently, from what he had gleaned at the mayor's dinner two weeks ago, his brother had traipsed all over the countryside to visit shareholders, managers and workers. How much better if they could all come to Eagle's Landing to conduct business—for the simple reason that Dalton would then know who the men were that he was to conduct business with!

Throwing down his pen with a frustrated growl, he rose from his chair and faced the window overlooking a stretch of tall firs and hardwoods that flanked the path leading into town.

He reasoned that after enough time elapsed and he didn't appear wherever he was supposed to go, they would come to him. But that hardly presented the confident acumen of one in control of the business. His mother daily assured him that she had faith he could do whatever was required, and he'd wryly begun to wonder if she also tried to convince herself. Not for the first time, he wished he had been trained alongside his brother. It was his father's great mistake that he never assumed the day would transpire when Dalton would claim the inheritance.

As he watched, the governess walked into view, the evening sun coaxing highlights of flame from her auburn hair. She came abreast of the path and looked down the road, pausing a short time before continuing her stroll.

He wondered if she also recalled the night, two weeks ago, when he almost trampled her with his horse. The terrifying encounter often came to mind, as did the forbidden kiss…a token of affection he had more than once wished to revisit, no matter how unwise. Once the urge had come over him after trying to shake sense into her head for her imprudent nighttime stroll in a coal-black cloak—he had wanted to embrace and kiss her soundly, in his relief to have her escape being crushed under sharp hooves. The next occasion, minutes afterward, she had looked so vulnerable and distressed trying to comfort her sister from a nightmare. Dalton had curbed the strong impulse to rush forward and give Myrna comfort, instead walking quickly away.

Closing his eyes, he bowed his head to the cool pane. Had he learned nothing from the past year with Giselle? And yet, the two women were nothing alike.

At first, he made the mistake of thinking so, but after dwelling on the matter of Myrna's deceit while in a composed state of mind, Dalton began to understand her reasoning. She was young, beautiful, struggling alone in a world that could be to her a danger, and she had her little sister's welfare to consider, as well. Giselle had been an only child raised in a lifestyle of plenty and could not offer the same excuse.

Muffled giggles told him he was no longer alone. He turned to face the two small girls who entered the room. His niece held a large volume clutched to her chest. Both children wore hopeful smiles.

"Rebecca. Sisi. I hope that you're not playing hide-and-seek from your governess again."

They exchanged a swift look, and Rebecca gave him a saucy grin. "Nana said you were busy all afternoon, but it's not afternoon anymore."

"No, indeed. It's almost suppertime. Would you like me to put that book back on the shelf for you?"

Rebecca shook her head and held the book out. "We

want you to read to us! Please, Uncle Dalton. You've been in here for hours and hours and *hours*."

He chuckled at his niece's exaggeration, though it did seem as if he'd been buried in the ledgers forever. A respite would be welcome.

Dalton accepted the large book. Embossed gold letters inscribed in a dark red leather cover showed that it was a collection of children's tales. "One story, then."

He sat on one of the winged armchairs in front of the fire glowing in the hearth. Rebecca wasted no time climbing onto his leg and, to his surprise, Sisi climbed onto the other. Putting his arms around both girls, he opened the book. Sisi laid her head against his neck.

"This one," Rebecca insisted, shuffling through pages to an area of the book that lay flatter, as though often read. "It's the one Papa used to read the most," she added sadly.

He squeezed his niece in comfort. "I doubt I can tell it as well as your papa," he said quietly, "but I'll give it my best."

# Chapter 9

Myrna walked into the manor, a little more clear-headed. It had become habitual to find solace in the chill but tranquil outdoors when an ache would start behind her eyes. The doctor's second visit neither appeased nor worried her. He left a tonic should the pain become intolerable, but so far she'd had no need of it, relying on Genevieve's wonderful hot mint teas, instead.

She walked into the parlor where the family usually met before dinner, finding no one there. Curious, she continued down the corridor and heard music coming from the conservatory. Peeking into the room, she spotted Mrs. Freed at the piano, but the girls, who had last been with her, were nowhere in sight.

Not wishing to interrupt Dalton's mother, Myrna went upstairs to look. Their bedchambers, the current playroom and her room were all empty.

Running across a maid, she stopped her. "Have you seen the girls?"

"They're in the library."

"Thank you, Daisy." Myrna continued downstairs, struggling against the fluttery sensation in her midsection as she neared the double doors. One stood ajar.

"'Oh, grandmother, what big eyes you have!'"

Myrna blinked in shock to hear Dalton's voice—altered to sound like a small girl. She pushed the door wide enough to peer into the room.

"'All the better to see you with.'"

This time his words came gruff, with a slight growl to them. Both girls sat comfortably in his lap. Rebecca giggled. Sisi stared up at his face in fascination, ignoring the book from which he read.

Again, he imitated a girl's voice. "'Oh, grandmother, what big hands you have!'"

"'All the better to grab you with!'" he growled and released the book to grab both girls closer to him. They squealed. Myrna smiled.

"'Oh, grandmother, what a horribly big mouth you have!'" A third time he spoke in a high falsetto voice.

"'All the better to eat you with!'" He snapped his teeth at both girls and repeatedly growled, earning more squeals as they pretended fear, making halfhearted efforts to slap at his arms and get away amid the laughter they couldn't keep from bubbling over.

"'And with that he jumped out of bed, jumped on top of poor Little Red Cap, and ate her up,'" he continued in his familiar tenor. "'As soon as the wolf had finished this tasty bite, he climbed back into bed, fell asleep, and began to snore very loudly…'"

The *wolf?* The gruff, villainous storybook character he'd been portraying was *a wolf?*

The irony proved too amusing and Myrna giggled.

Alerted to her presence, Dalton and the girls looked her way. He closed the book.

"That's it for tonight, girls."

"But what about Little Red Cap?" Sisi asked worriedly. "Did she die?"

"Please, do finish the story." Myrna moved into the room and took the opposite chair. "You must never leave a story unfinished. It's the cardinal rule of storytelling. Pay me no mind. You won't even notice me." Smiling innocently, she couldn't resist using against him the same words he had said to her in this same room.

His mouth twisted wryly and he narrowed his eyes at her, as if sensing her true wish to be part of the audience, but he opened the book and resumed. She listened as he then became the huntsman who cut the wolf open and saved Little Red Cap and her grandmother, marveling at his take on yet another accent and voice, German this time, and trying hard not to laugh at again hearing him speak as the little girl. His eyes suspiciously flicked to her a few times when she covered her smile with her hand or quenched back a helpless chuckle. Once the tale of the wolf's demise concluded, Rebecca looked at Dalton in expectation.

"And...?" his niece prodded.

"And...?" Dalton looked at her, mystified.

"You're supposed to say what the moral of the tale is."

"Don't talk to wolves dressed in ruffled nightgowns and bed caps?" he guessed with a shrug.

Myrna laughed outright, and he directed another narrow-eyed glance her way.

"I suppose you can do better?"

"I heard only the tail end of the tale," she quipped.

He winced at the poor pun, and they both smiled.

Rebecca exhaled a disgusted sigh, crossing her arms over her blue-sprigged bodice as if she was the teacher regarding her dense pupils. "The moral is that young girls should never trust strangers nor talk to them 'cause they may become a wolf's dinner. Papa said so."

"Ah, I see. I agree with your papa. Speaking of dinner, it's nearing that time."

He set the book on the floor then helped Sisi and Rebecca off his lap. Sisi ran to Myrna and hugged her happily, motioning for her to bend down so she could whisper in her ear.

Sisi cupped her hands around her mouth. "I like Uncle Dalton. He's nice."

Myrna straightened to look at her smiling sister, not bothering to correct his relationship to her, since it had done no good the many times she tried.

"Shall we?"

Dalton approached. Rebecca grabbed Sisi's hand and together they left the room in quiet discussion over the story. Dalton offered Myrna his arm and noticed her hesitation.

"We've had a number of false starts. Perhaps we should put those mistakes behind us and begin anew?"

His eyes regarded her with warmth—kind, but with an intensity that always left her a bit breathless—and unable to resist, she took his arm.

"Where have I heard that before?" she teased.

He softly chuckled. "I haven't the slightest idea."

She smiled, feeling at ease with him for the first time in a long while. She had thought him a wolf when they first met, wary to trust his motives, but almost two months in his household had shown her a side to Dalton she hadn't expected. Perhaps, given her shattered history, she'd been wrong to judge in haste. He had his faults, so did she, and a few mirrored his.

For the most part, he behaved more like the huntsman of the tale, rescuing her and her sister, giving them nothing but aid. He had won over Sisi, and she did not give her trust easily, a flawed trait Myrna had unwittingly passed on to her. She wanted her sister to know happiness and not always be fearful of what worries the next day would bring or who would bring them.

With that resolve, Myrna was willing to accept his extended truce, to see where it led. Thus, once she tucked the girls in for the night, afterward taking the stairs down to the foyer, Myrna regarded him with polite curiosity when he walked into view as she reached the landing.

He drew his brows together to see her dark cloak. "You're going out?"

"I've made it a nightly custom to engage in a stroll before I turn in. It helps to clear my head."

"Do you mind if I join you?"

"I promise not to walk in the middle of the road, and I won't go without a lantern."

His lips flickered at the corners. "A wise choice. But you didn't answer. May I join you?"

For an astonished heartbeat she regarded him with surprise that he would want to, then faintly nodded her consent. She moved in the direction of the corridor leading to the kitchen. He stopped her, his hand touching her arm.

"Where are you going?"

"To the back entrance."

"When the front door is only yards away?"

"Miss Browning told me the servants are always to use the back door, and I'm only the governess."

He looked at her, his expression grave. "You may use whatever entrance you wish. Come."

His hand at her elbow was firm as he led her toward the front double doors. He took a lantern from the wall that had been hanging out of sight behind a coatrack and lit it.

"We keep it there for emergencies," he explained. "Feel free to use it if you need it."

He opened the door and held the lantern outside, lighting her path. "After you," he said with a flourish of his other hand.

Their walk together was the first of what soon became a ritual, a peaceful time for candid conversation, where for the length of a stroll, he ceased being her employer, and in his company she considered herself more than a governess. Magical minutes where they spoke as equals, reminisced of fond memories and even laughed together, and by the end of the week, Myrna realized the unthinkable had happened.

She had come to care for the master of Eagle's Landing.

By the following week, she knew her heart was in a perilous state and strongly suspected her feelings were evolving into something beyond mere caring.

But for once, she did not talk herself out of it.

A week and a half later, Dalton walked beside Myrna as they strolled through the garden still in the throes of new life. Gravely she considered what she'd heard. She and Sisi had gone with the Freeds to attend church services that morning, as they'd been doing for some time. The memory of today's message gave her pause.

"Something troubles you."

Dalton's quiet voice broke the stillness of the evening and startled her into awareness that she had indeed been brooding. "The minister spoke of wolves in sheep's clothing." It seemed she would forever be haunted by the prospect of wolves. "How is it that we can discern an enemy if he becomes so close that we think him a friend?"

"I understood from the message that we should draw that much closer to God, so that deception wouldn't be possible. We would then hear the Shepherd's voice, and be warned in the event of approaching danger."

"But how is that possible?" She glanced his way.

"I was taught that God speaks to the hearts of those who

draw near to Him." He was quiet a moment and she mulled over his words. "Do you still think of me as a wolf?"

Her eyes went huge and she snapped her attention to him.

"Why would you ask such a thing?" she breathed.

"Don't tell me the thought never crossed your mind," he said calmly. "We both know otherwise."

"We do?" Feeling adrift in the conversation, her heart beating fast at the unexpected mild attack, she waited to hear what he would say.

"The night I brought you here, when you were injured, you spoke out when we were tending you."

She laughed nervously. "I actually looked into your eyes and called you a wolf?" she asked, highly doubting it.

"As a matter of fact, yes."

"Oh." She looked back at the path, unable to speak beyond that one syllable.

"The question being," he went on with calm persistence, "do you still regard me as one?"

Carefully she framed her answer. "If I did, I don't suppose I would be taking these strolls with you in the dark of the night."

He smiled. "No, I don't suppose so. Now tell me, I am most curious. Why do you prefer nighttime strolls to those taken in daylight?"

"With the girls tucked safely in their beds, I can take that sliver of time for myself. The evening is peaceful. With the lantern you carry, I feel safe." It was more than the bobbing glow of golden light that made her feel protected; it was the company kept, but she wasn't yet ready to admit her delight in having him near.

"Are you not content with your position as governess?"

"Oh, yes! I didn't mean to imply otherwise. But the task is endless and I'm still learning my role." They approached a stone bench near the pond. Myrna hesitated. "I'd like to rest."

"Of course."

She sat down, leaning a little sideways with one hand on the bench to look out over the still, black water. He hung the lantern from a branch above and took a seat beside her.

"It's lovely here," she breathed in appreciation.

"Then you do believe you could find happiness at Eagle's Landing?"

At his odd question, she glanced at him. He didn't look at her but stared straight ahead at the manor.

"For Sisi's sake, I'll try." Her words came as quietly as his. A gradual shift seemed to affect the atmosphere, bringing her senses into heightened awareness. "I've come to realize it's what's best for her."

"But not for you?"

She didn't know how to answer, so kept silent.

"It is highly commendable, the care you exhibit toward your sister." He looked at her then. "And Rebecca enjoys having you as her governess. Other than when it comes to her studies, of course."

Myrna felt grateful for his levity and change of subject. "She doesn't like arithmetic."

"I didn't, either, when I was her age. Now it's translations that have become the banc of my existence." At her curious stare, he explained, "The estate ledgers. My brother failed to write with a steady hand."

Recalling her own experience, she nodded. "I sympathize. My father— Oh!"

Feeling the tickle of something crawl along her jaw, she whisked her fingers there.

"Are you all right?"

She brushed her fingertips over her neck at the ghost traces and the certainty she had not rid herself of the mysterious, vile creature.

"A bug." She felt suddenly as if they were crawling all over her and jumped to stand. "I hope it's not a spider!" She detested the eight-legged beasts.

"Calm yourself. It was likely a gnat or mosquito."

She felt the tickle again, near her ear this time, and batted her fingers in that area.

He rose and took hold of her head at the back. His other hand tilted her face to the lantern light while he inspected her features. Shivers of a different sort whispered across her skin at the touch of his warm fingertips brushing the side of her neck and barely stroking her scalp. His last movements came more slowly as he trailed the contour of her jaw.

"Whatever was there has gone."

At the low timbre of his voice, she found it difficult to look into his eyes. In the next moment, she found it impossible not to. Lifting her gaze to his, she noted the dark intensity she had glimpsed before, again making her breathless as they stared at one another for endless moments. His thumb ghosted across her parted lips. She felt fixed, unable to move, barely able to breathe as he tilted her chin higher. Her eyes fell shut as his mouth touched hers.

She exhaled her breath in a rush but did not retreat. Neither did she push him away.

His kiss tasted of cloves and cinnamon, engendering feelings of warmth and protection…and more. Frozen by his unexpected affection, at the same time she felt as if she stood close to a gentle hearth blaze. A second brush of his lips against hers seemed to free her to move, and she returned his kiss, lifting her hands to press against his waistcoat, the cloth rough beneath the pads of her fingertips, the sensation of his heartbeats, as rapid as hers, making them tingle.

He softly broke the kiss, pulling away to look into her

eyes. The expression in their gray depths was as stunned as she felt.

"That's the second time you've done that," she breathed.

"This time I'll not apologize."

It would be foolish, since by her keen response she had revealed her pleasure.

"But…why…?" Her question remained unfinished, her equilibrium shaky.

"I've come to care for you, Myrna."

The rush of warmth his husky words provoked led to another at the familiar use of her name, the first time he had used it. Old fears resurfaced. She took a step back.

"What is it you want from me?"

At her nervous words, he studied her face. His eyes were clear in their sincerity—no dark, hidden motive lurking beneath. He gave her a nonthreatening smile, rare to see and boyish in its charm. She found herself wishing to initiate more like it.

"I don't want anything. I suggest we take each day in stride, to see where this leads us."

"How can it lead anywhere?" she whispered. "Our lives are so very different—"

Her words abruptly halted in surprise at the brief touch of his two fingers against her lips.

"Don't. Those things don't matter to me, but perhaps it's too soon to have this conversation. At this time, I wish only for your continued companionship. I've enjoyed our nighttime strolls."

At the question in his eyes, Myrna nodded, having enjoyed them as well but embarrassed that she'd spoken so freely.

He reached up to collect the lantern then held out his arm. "We should return to the manor."

She slipped her hand around his elbow, relieved to find mutual harmony, which they had been working toward with their cease-fire of eleven days. Yet the question remained. Despite many roadblocks—their different stations in life, her family scandal, what she'd once overheard about him, their difficulty to trust each other—could there ever be more for them?

The odds seemed stacked against their favor, and Myrna knew she was foolish to hope. But in the warmth of his presence it was easy to cling to the frailty of dreams.

## Chapter 10

"Eck! You stay there, Uncle Dalton. Don't come inside," Rebecca warned, closing the door behind her and dramatically spreading her arms to bar his entrance into the closed dining room.

After concluding his work early he had walked to the dining room that Rebecca just exited. A room evidently off-limits. He withheld a chuckle, wondering what surprise the girls and his mother had in store. He couldn't resist a bit of teasing.

"My dear niece, it's time for the meal and I wish to be prompt. What kind of message would I send if I taught you never to be tardy and then didn't do likewise?"

"You can be late for one day," she argued.

"I would rather not tempt the habit to start."

She crossed her arms over her chest, her jaw set stubbornly.

He rubbed his chin with his forefinger and thumb and

pretended to contemplate the matter. "Would a kiss on thy hand be adequate to pay the toll?"

She giggled then grew stern again. "*I'm* the toll master and I say you may not enter."

The door opened behind her.

She let out another shriek, grabbing Myrna's arm to pull her through and hastily closing the door. Myrna's surprise to be treated thus evaporated on catching sight of Dalton.

"I told him he can't go inside," Rebecca said, "but he's being difficult."

"Difficult? Alas, no. I'm willing to barter, sweet maiden. What might I give in return for crossing the forbidden threshold?"

Myrna's lips twitched. A trace of mischief gleamed in his niece's eyes.

"I think, to cross, you must kiss the hand...*of the governess!*"

At Rebecca's boisterous command, a becoming flush glowed on Myrna's cheeks.

A month ago, even a week, Dalton would never have dared. Ten days had changed much between them since his second impromptu kiss, and their friendship had strengthened. With that in mind, he caught Myrna's eye, giving her a mischievous smirk.

"Since the toll mistress decrees it, I must obey," he said by way of explanation.

"The girl has become a wretched slave to a stranger's charm." Myrna seemed equal parts amused and somber, her words coming wryly. "A foolish thing, if she will recall the moral of a recent wolf's tale."

Rebecca giggled. "Uncle Dalton's no stranger! And he's not a wolf, either."

"The girl speaks correctly," he said in blithe defense.

"But not always wisely. Very well. We wouldn't wish to upset the toll mistress."

Curbing a chuckle, he took her extended hand in his and bent over it, barely brushing the pale, unblemished skin with a kiss and eliciting a louder giggle from his niece.

"I think the traveler has paid his due," Myrna said with a smile, their eyes meeting as he lifted his gaze.

Rebecca looked at her. "But Nana said—"

"It's all right," Myrna reassured, softly pulling back her hand that Dalton released with reluctance.

Before he could finally gain entrance, Miss Browning hurried their way.

"Beggin' your pardon, sir, there's a visitor to see you."

"We were just going in to dinner."

"I told him, but he's insistent on seeing you. Said it was important he speak with the master who runs the place."

"It's likely one of those in the books whose name is still a mystery."

At Myrna's evident confusion, he smiled dryly. "I'll explain later. I had best go see what he wants. Go ahead and start without me."

"But we can't, Uncle Dalton! Not today—"

"I'll tell your mother." Myrna took hold of Rebecca's arm, steering her into the dining room.

With an irritated sigh to have his meal disturbed, Dalton headed toward the foyer.

"Do you think he'll like it?" Rebecca asked nervously.

"Yes, I think he will." Myrna double-checked the table to make sure nothing had been missed.

"He's coming!" Sisi announced from her self-appointed post by the door, and Rebecca hurried to the opposite side to wait.

No more than five minutes had passed since Dalton was detained, and the steam rising from the dishes proved the meal was still hot. After sharing a smile with Mrs. Freed who sat at the foot of the table, Myrna returned her attention to the door.

It opened and the girls threw handfuls of the confetti they had shredded toward Dalton, showering him with snippets of white.

"Happy birthday!" they cried.

A stranger walked in behind him, also getting bombarded by the minuscule paper shower. A tall, slender man approximately the same age as Dalton, the visitor didn't look at all happy to receive the welcome. Briskly he brushed the shredded bits from his curly brown hair and one that clung to his thick mustache.

The celebratory atmosphere turned quizzical as almost everyone in the room looked at the newcomer. By the expression on Dalton's face as he stared only at Myrna, she felt the first prickling of dread.

"I would like to speak with you a moment in the parlor," he said quietly.

Ignoring Dalton's words, the stranger walked around him and approached. "You are Myrna? Yes? That bright hair gives you away. I'm your cousin, Jeremy."

Sisi ran to Myrna and clutched her skirts, eyeing the newcomer in apprehension.

"I would prefer that we speak in the parlor." Dalton's firm words came from the doorway, and Myrna snapped out of her haze of shock.

"Yes, all right." She smoothed her hand down Sisi's head. "You stay here with Rebecca and Mrs. Freed and be a good girl."

She smiled at her sister and barely offered a glance toward Jeremy as she joined Dalton. The three moved to the smaller room.

"If you'd give me a moment with my cousin," Jeremy said to Dalton.

"No," Myrna said. "I wish him to stay."

Jeremy looked at her as if affronted, but she didn't know or trust him so didn't retract her statement. Grumbling a little, he walked toward her, pulling an envelope from his waistcoat. She looked at the missive as if it might grow fangs and bite.

"These are your father's instructions to me, a letter he sent two years ago."

Still, she refused to take it, lifting her cautious gaze to his dark one. "I sent a post after the accident, informing you of my change in plans. Did you not receive it?"

His brown eyes were somber. "It's the reason I came. Take it, Myrna."

She accepted the missive but didn't open it.

He sighed. "Your father wrote me that should he die and you contact me for help, it was his wish that I take care of you and your sister. To marry you—it's in the letter," he added when she gasped in shocked distress at the last of what he said.

Inadvertently, her eyes went to Dalton. He stared back, his expression grim but not surprised, and she wondered if Jeremy had already told him.

"But you're family," she whispered. "I couldn't possibly…"

"Nothing wrong with cousins marrying. The gentry does it all the time." Jeremy shook his head. "Still, your father never told you the details of our relationship? My father and your father were brothers, but I was adopted. We're not blood kin."

The blood pounded in Myrna's head. "But—I can't leave. I'm the governess."

"You would deny your father's wishes? I'm sure they can find another nanny." He stared at her as if he expected her to run upstairs, pack her bag and leave with him straightaway.

She felt uncertain of the right thing to do. To go with

this cousin she had never known and entrust their lives to him. Or to stay with the family who welcomed her, where she and Sisi had found peace and a measure of happiness…

"I need time to think about it," she said weakly.

"I don't understand," he argued, stepping closer as if to grab her. "I thought you were coming on the train to see me."

"The lady said she needs time." Dalton's cool words sliced through the chill air.

Jeremy glanced his way, took in his tall form, leaner but more muscular than her cousin's, then looked back at Myrna. "An hour, then?"

"I couldn't possibly make such a decision tonight! I have a position here. Much has changed. Sisi is happy."

"Are you telling me my trip was for nothing?"

She wrung her hands in her skirts. "I'm sorry, I don't know what to tell you. This is all so sudden."

"You're welcome to stay as our guest, if Miss McBride desires your presence," Dalton said genially, though the words seemed torn from him as stilted as they came.

"Yes, that would be lovely," she said in haste. "Thank you, Mr. Freed."

"I left my shop in my apprentice's care," Jeremy hedged. "I can't be absent for long."

"Then you should return. Once I make my decision, if it is to—to abide by the letter, Sisi and I will travel to your home then."

At her hurried and awkward suggestion, he looked back and forth between Myrna and Dalton, as if in sudden realization. "I can take a short time away."

"I'll have my driver collect your things in town."

"I only have the one satchel I left by the door."

"Very well. I'll have a maid take it to your room."

"Maids in the corridors. Drivers at your beck and call. Dear cousin, are you sure you've not had your head turned by such luxuries and that is why you won't give me an immediate answer?"

Myrna's face heated at his overtly rude statement and familiar form of address.

"Miss McBride said she needs time," Dalton stressed again. "We should respect her wishes." His eyes went to Myrna. "For now, we should return to the dining hall. They'll wonder what's keeping us."

"Sounds good," Jeremy said. "I'm starved."

Myrna shared a somber look with Dalton as the three left the parlor. This certainly wasn't how she had planned his birthday celebration.

"Are you all right?" he asked, low enough for her ears only.

She looked at him then away, loath to say yes and lie and just as averse to say no and burden him with her problems.

Myrna ate little, appalled by Jeremy's table manners, if he was ever taught such niceties. Sitting directly across from him, she couldn't help notice. He talked with his mouth full, chewed with his mouth open, reached for platters and took exorbitant servings and huge bites. The girls gawked at him. They glanced her way, and Myrna shook her head a little in rebuke not to stare. For all that, the man was engaging, now that the awkward introductions were behind them, and he answered and asked questions with ease, speaking of his clockmaker's shop with enthusiasm.

The man of honor, for which this special meal had been prepared, remained quiet through all four courses of his favorite foods, though Myrna was relieved to see that he did eat. Their eyes met now and again, each incident sending little flutters through her middle, especially during those moments when neither looked away for a time.

Afterward, cake was served, and the girls, excited again, rushed to Dalton with their presents. He thanked Rebecca for her hand drawing of Eagle's Landing, with depictions of all of them outside on a summer's day, promising to frame and hang it near his desk. The child was gifted, the drawing that she had worked on for days true to form.

He opened the paper parcel Sisi handed him and withdrew a handkerchief. Dark blue trim had been embroidered around the edges, his initials in matching thread at a corner.

"You did this?"

"Actually, it was Myrna," Sisi admitted. "But I wrapped it."

"And it was beautifully done," he assured her.

Myrna felt a wash of warmth as his curious gaze swung her way.

"I did some needlework in the past," she said. "It's to replace the one I took."

Memory of the kiss that followed made it hard to breathe. By the intent manner in which he stared, she wondered if he recalled that intimate occasion.

"I thought you worked as a librarian." Jeremy disrupted the moment. "It's what you wrote."

She nervously fiddled with the stem of her goblet, realized she did so, then pulled her hand away. "I did assist at the Astor Library, but only for the first months of its opening."

"Better than the textile mills from what I hear," he concluded.

"That was never an option." Her focus went to Sisi, who never would have survived if Myrna had secured a job at one of the mills. Likely Sisi would have been forced to work alongside her. Myrna wouldn't have left her sister alone in the tenement for such long hours. Her former neighbors, a mother with a daughter four years older than Sisi, worked at the mills from sunup to past sundown every day, and she had often listened to their accounts of atrocious working conditions and watched as their health deteriorated through the year.

Had Myrna chosen such a path, her sister might be dead now.

"I make my home above my shop, but it's small, so you won't have much to do," Jeremy said. "You'll take care of the upkeep of both places and greet my customers, assisting me as needed."

At his sudden enthused summarization of her life, Myrna felt trapped.

"I haven't agreed to go with you," she stated quietly, wishing to conclude the topic with little fuss and much haste. "As I said, there's much to consider."

"Just letting you know how things will be, to help you decide."

To her surprise, Sisi walked up to her chair and motioned for Myrna to bend down. Her little sister cupped her hand around Myrna's ear. "I don't like him," she whispered. "He looks like the wolf."

With the present company sitting across from her, now was hardly the time for such a discussion. She looked at Sisi. "We'll talk about this later."

*Later* came that night as she tucked Sisi into bed.

"Why did he come?" she asked, frowning.

"He's our cousin."

"I don't like him. He has big teeth like the wolf in the story."

He did have big teeth, but the rest of his features worked well together to give a pleasing appearance. After his initial introduction, he had been kind, so Myrna didn't understand her sister's strong abhorrence.

"I like Uncle Dalton. He looks better and acts nicer."

Myrna agreed but didn't air that aloud, either. "Jeremy is family. We should give him a chance," she gently chided, pulling the blanket to her sister's chin. "I want you to be nice to him."

Sisi nodded reluctantly, and Myrna kissed her goodnight. Once in her own room, she finally opened the letter with trembling hands and sank to her bed. She read her father's shaky scrawl three times. It was all there, as Jeremy said.

Father had asked her unknown cousin to help if she should contact him once Father passed away, lauding her abilities and that she would make a good wife. Writing that it would be beneficial for them to marry, he followed with his request that Jeremy take care of both Myrna and Sisi.

"Oh, Papa," Myrna lamented, wishing now that she'd never written to her cousin.

Her father had only been looking out for her welfare. Myrna knew that, but marriage for her was inconceivable, or at least it had been....

Her tentative friendship with Dalton had evolved into something more precious, though neither of them acted on the difference or spoke of it. He never again tried to kiss her, but she sensed the shift between them, with the soft, intent way he would sometimes look at her...the gentle touches to her arm or shoulder when he would move past... the little nuances that caused her heart to beat like the fragile wings of a butterfly.

Not that it mattered. Their worlds were too differing in extremes, and she belonged to the one her cousin offered. Still, Myrna resisted her father's wishes, not yet reconciled to make the decision that would tear her and Sisi away from Eagle's Landing. Weeks ago, to escape this place and the master who ran it was her fondest hope, the letter a coveted link to bequeath that objective. But now...

If Myrna didn't feel ready to weep at the misfortune so suddenly cast her way, she would laugh at the irony.

# Chapter 11

The following morning, Jeremy joined Myrna and the girls in the sunny nook where they took their breakfasts. Neither Rebecca nor Sisi looked pleased to see him, but to their credit they did not misbehave or stare at his bad table manners.

Afterward, the girls had planned an hour with Mrs. Freed before lessons, and they scampered out of the room, leaving Myrna alone with Jeremy. Before she could make a polite excuse and go, he stopped her, walking fast ahead of her to the door and blocking her escape.

"I don't have an answer for you yet," she said quickly.

"I wanted this chance to talk alone. Don't be upset." He shook his head in confusion. "I thought you wanted to come to me. Your first letter implied it. You took the train."

"Yes, but as I told you in the telegram, much has changed since then. And I was coming to be with family. Not to be a wife."

He lifted his brows slightly and stared as if her words

held no significance. "Your telegram alarmed me, which is why I came to investigate."

"You had no cause for alarm."

"Didn't I?"

"What do you mean?" she asked, flustered.

"You're a governess here, Myrna, and a governess is all you'll ever be. Is that what your father wanted for you? To serve *the wealthy* and live as a servant? After what happened to your family?"

"I can't think about this right now," she hedged, wondering how much he knew. "I have to prepare lessons."

He put up his hands in a placating manner. "Forgive my impatience, but I expected you here waiting for me. Seems like I'm the one who must do the waiting, for you to see reason."

His tone came quiet and undemanding, but she felt cornered.

"There's much to consider," she said for what seemed like the hundredth time. "You are my cousin, and I was traveling to be with our family. What you are proposing now is much different. Here, Sisi is happy—"

"Sisi's a child. She can be happy elsewhere. Are you sure there isn't more holding you back?" he mused. "These people aren't like us, Myrna. We're family. We have to stick together."

Myrna felt fatigued with the subject. "Please, not now. I must go."

"All right. But ask yourself how your parents would feel if they knew you were in a position like your mother once was."

Her head snapped up in horror. "You know about that?"

"That wasn't your father's only letter. I discovered the rest of your history when I wrote to your former employer at the library."

"You wrote to Mr. Jenkins?" Embarrassed heat warmed her face. She could frame no answer.

He nodded once. "Do the Freeds know about the old scandal? About Sisi? About the trouble you found yourself in last year?" At her continued silence, he grimaced. "If they did you wouldn't still be in service. The wealthy thrive on reputation, you know. It's their daily bread. Think on that, Myrna."

With that, he moved aside.

Troubled, she hurried past him and out the door.

Dalton looked at the square parchment his mother had brought to him earlier.

The preparations for the spring ball that his family hosted each May had begun. He had shown frank surprise upon hearing that his mother still planned to host the event this year, but understood her expressed wish to reach out to their town and bring the people together in a cheerful atmosphere.

"There's been enough grief and death in this house for some time to come," she had told him. "I've had enough. It's time for change. If I make the social faux pas of the century by throwing a ball in my time of mourning and tongues start to wag, so be it."

Dalton fondly smiled. As beloved as his mother was to the populace, offering her help or a listening ear, he doubted the citizens of Hillsdale would regard her unkindly. Some age-old traditions were meant to be broken, and to see his mother excited about a project again was worth every bit of censure he might receive from those dogged to custom.

The door opened, and Myrna stepped inside. Seeing him, she hesitated.

He motioned her forward. "Please, come in. I've been looking over an invitation to a ball our family is holding."

"A ball?" she asked, approaching his desk.

"Yes, in four weeks." He handed her the placard. "What do you think?"

She studied the script and handed it back. "You might wish to add an apostrophe to 'evening's entertainment.' Otherwise, it looks lovely."

He stared at the invitation, noting she was correct about the missing punctuation. "You have sharp eyesight." An idea occurred, one his mother had teasingly alluded to weeks ago, but now he wished to put to the test. Opening his brother's ledger, he turned to the page he'd been unable to decipher, and handed her the book. "Can you read this?"

"Oh, my."

He grimaced. "My thoughts exactly."

"You own a textile mill?" Her eyes snapped to his. "Isn't that like a factory?"

"It's the same concept, machines that mass produce, but not on such a grand scale." He stared at her. "You can actually read that?"

"Yes. It's a basic report of a recent visit there and the conditions, including those of the workers, along with a brief accounting of financial profit with the manager, Thomas Orley. And a few lines about the need to replace some machinery."

Dalton gaped at her in amazement then grabbed his new ledger and a pen, dipping it in the bottle of ink. "If you wouldn't mind reciting word for word while I transfer it to these pages?"

"Of course." She seemed tense, but smiled and took the seat across from him. For the next several minutes, her soft voice unveiled the mystery of months. He took the book from her, quickly ruffling to another page.

"I've made out the names of those with an asterisk beside them, but others I cannot decipher. Also the places of locale next to their names. If you wouldn't mind?"

Again she cited while he jotted.

"It is uncanny how alike this is to my father's writing," she mused. "He didn't always pen all of his vowels, either, and his scrawl was just as shaky."

"You have been most helpful, Myrna. A true godsend." As he spoke, he used the blotter to soak up excess ink then turned his eyes up to her. He thought it enchanting how her cheeks flushed with rose at his compliment. "I can at last lay this business to rest and act upon what I have learned."

Her smile was feeble at best. "This mill you own, from what the account said, the working conditions are poor...."

He nodded for her to go on when she hesitated.

"I had neighbors who worked at a factory with poor working conditions. A mother and her daughter. A child. The girl developed a horrid cough that never ceased. Both grew ill, though they continued to work long hours."

He leaned forward. "I value human life above all else. You have no cause for concern. I'll look into this and do all within my power to ensure that our working conditions are safe for all."

Her smile again was faint but seemed more genuine. "I believe you." Her words came soft and wondering, as if she just realized they were true.

Dalton knew how difficult it was for her to trust and felt as though he'd won a small victory. He picked up the placard. "I must drive into town and drop this off at the printer's. I'll stop in at the mill on my way home."

"And I should collect the book I came to get for the girls' lesson." She rose from her chair.

"Tell me," he said thoughtfully before she could walk away, "do you know how to waltz?"

"Waltz?" She blinked, taken aback by the question. "No, I was never taught."

"Then I shall look forward to teaching you...at the ball," he added when she looked blankly at him.

"According to the invitation, that's a little over four weeks away."

"Yes?"

"I might not be here then."

"Where would you go?" At the memory of their unwanted guest, he sobered and moved around his desk toward her. "You cannot seriously consider leaving us to go with your cousin?"

"It's what my father wanted." She sounded discontented.

"You think you would be happy stuffed in a shop, dusting clocks all day long?"

"What other option do I have?"

"A home, here, with us."

She looked impatient with the conversation. "As I told Jeremy, I've not yet decided. Now, if you'll excuse me, I really must go."

She hurried past him. He remained fixed, frustrated with the situation and wishing he had never agreed to send a telegraph to her cousin. He didn't think it was only resentment at the man's sudden appearance that led to his suspicions that Jeremy McBride was no wise choice for Myrna.

The days stretched into a week. Still, Myrna gave Jeremy no answer, haunted by his reminder of her family's scandal but still not ready to leave what had become a haven in her storm. Or, truth be told, Dalton.

In the second week, Sisi grew sick with a bad cold. Myrna kept up lessons with Rebecca and spent the rest of her time doting on her bedridden sister. Jeremy sent a telegram to his shop, receiving in return a wire from his apprentice stating that nothing had come up he couldn't handle, but he would contact him if it did. Thus assured, Jeremy settled into life at Eagle's Landing.

"Hello." Mrs. Freed's voice came from the doorway.

Myrna smiled and set down the book she'd been reading—the fourth time now. The complicated friendship of Jane and Mr. Rochester intrigued her, and she wondered how Jane knew it had become more than that for her, turning into love.

"Please, come in," she invited.

"I see that she's sleeping." Mrs. Freed smiled fondly at Sisi then turned her gaze to Myrna. "But have you slept?"

"Here and there. She's doing much better." The soreness in Sisi's throat had disappeared and the cough also dwindled. Thankfully, according to Dr. Clark it wasn't Pertussis, which had been Myrna's greatest fear, since Sisi had been struck with the ailment as a child.

"Might I have a word with you in your room?"

Curious, Myrna rose from her chair and followed the older woman.

In her bedchamber, she looked with puzzlement at the array of colorful gowns on the bed.

"I hope you don't mind that I took the liberty." Mrs. Freed picked up a dress of shimmering mauve. "With the ball only a little over two weeks away, there's no time to secure a new dress, but you look about the size that Roger's wife was. Shorter in height, but Genevieve can adjust the hem. Thankfully, the gowns are still considered the mode of fashion."

Myrna shook her head in a slight daze as the woman swept toward her and held the dress to her form with a practiced eye. "Hmm. Perhaps the green." She replaced the blue in her arms for an emerald silk.

"Has Mr. Freed not spoken to you? I don't know if I'll be here for the ball."

"But you haven't yet reached a decision? So you'll be prepared if you should decide in our favor. I admit freely that I hope you'll stay, Myrna. It's been lovely engaging in our parlor chats. Try this one."

Feeling powerless under such determination, Myrna allowed the woman to help her exchange her day dress for the ball gown. Mrs. Freed fluffed the many flounces and studied her.

"Lovely. We need go no further. The gown will require hemming, and you'll need a wider hoop, easily obtained... Come, see what you think." She brought her to stand before the looking glass.

Myrna gaped at her reflection, the expensive gown flattering her high coloring and making her feel like a princess. "But I'm only the governess," she whispered, not having meant to air the words.

"And certainly the most lovely governess in the state," Mrs. Freed said with a smile at her reflection. "Don't allow simple titles to cloud the worth of who you are as an individual, Myrna. There's no dishonor in teaching and caring for the children of others."

Soothed by her words, Myrna asked the question haunting her for weeks. "How do you know when a decision is the right one to make?"

"The light of it warms your heart," Mrs. Freed said without hesitation. "Once made, the knowledge becomes a part of you, and you realize all is as it should be." She squeezed her shoulders. "I know that you're in a difficult place. Perhaps you think it's unfair of me to try to persuade you to stay—at least for the ball. In the end, however, I want what's best for both you and Sisi and pray that God will grant you the wisdom to understand what that is."

Myrna glanced at her altered reflection, wishing but doubting the answer would be so uncomplicated. Her life had never been simple, and despite her employer's encouragement, Myrna doubted that would change.

# Chapter 12

Playing the congenial host, Dalton remained beside his hostess mother in her black taffeta that rustled with every movement as they revolved about the room and received their guests. All of the upper and middle class in Hillsdale and the surrounding county were annually invited for the event, and the turnout was always strong. Smiling and engaging in conversation, with the musicians playing softly in the background, his mother was in her element, and he could easily see how she'd once been the belle of the ball. Yet she had endured much in the past year alone, and the strain was soon evident at the corners of her mouth.

After speaking to a professor at Hillsdale about her desire to provide financial aid for worthy nurses with academic merit and low income to be trained at the college, her latest pet project since the train disaster, she was escorted by Dalton to a chair on the sidelines.

"My dear boy, whatever are you doing?" she asked, but took a seat, seeming grateful for it.

"Taking care that you don't overextend yourself as you are wont to do at these affairs."

She waved her black lace fan and smiled. "Oh, very well. I shall be content to sit here and watch as I planned to do all along. But *you* must mingle with the guests."

"Would you care for some refreshment first?"

"Go, Dalton. If I'm in need of punch, I'll ask someone to come to my aid." Even as she spoke, he noticed the bank owner and his wife move toward her, old friends of the family.

Being sociable among the multitudes was never his strong suit, but with a gracious nod to the arriving guests, Dalton set his jaw and moved through the throngs, hoping to see only one face.

In the semi-crowded foyer, his desire was at last rewarded as he lifted his eyes to the staircase and watched beauty descend the steps in green silk. He held his breath at the sight. The gown brought out the vivid green of her eyes, making them shimmer like emeralds, full of mystique. Her hair had been swept upward, a waterfall of bright auburn curls rippling down one side. Even the spray of faint freckles across her nose and dotting the apples of her cheeks he found enchanting.

"Miss McBride." He approached as she moved down the last steps and spoke so only she could hear. "You are a vision. I am pleased that you didn't change your mind."

She gave him a nervous smile. "It took me a while to persuade Sisi to go to sleep. She wanted to be here."

He grinned. "Ah, yes. It is the dream of young children prohibited from such social events. I remember peeking through the balcony rails with Alyssa to watch the guests."

On recent walks together he told her about memories of his little sister. Visiting her bedchamber, where the girls had been hiding, and later seeing Myrna in the abandoned playroom had left him shaken and distressed. Later it resurrected the need to speak of Alyssa, with Myrna, who cared so much about her own sister. But his last memory of Alyssa was still too painful to recall. He had never yet been able to speak of her death, though Myrna had asked.

"I can picture it." She flicked her eyes to the second landing. "And I wouldn't be at all surprised if two small girls get it into their heads to do the same. I shall have to keep an eye out for such mischief."

"Oh, let them be. It can cause no harm. Would you care to dance?"

Her smile faded and she nervously looked toward the open doors of the crowded ballroom. "I couldn't. I don't know the steps, and I don't wish to learn them among so many."

He nodded in understanding. "Would you care for some punch, then? Cake, perhaps?"

"Yes, please." Her eyes sparkled as she took his proffered arm. "I couldn't help notice the delicious aromas wafting from the kitchen all morning. Though I don't wish to keep you from your guests...."

"Myrna, there you are." Jeremy's voice accosted them from the corridor.

Dalton tensed, his hand closing more tightly over Myrna's gloved fingers that rested on his arm.

The persistent clockmaker approached. "Quite the affair," he enthused, nodding to Dalton then looking at Myrna. "Glad you convinced me to stay. Never been to anything like it. I found another of my trade and want you to meet him, my dear."

Dalton sharply looked at her, noting the heightened flush of her cheeks. She had *convinced* her cousin to stay *and wait?* Meaning she had come closer to a decision to leave them?

Jeremy grabbed her arm and bustled her away, leaving Dalton to stare after the pair.

Grimacing, he turned, coming face-to-face with some-one he thought never to see again.

"Dalton," Giselle said quietly, closing the short distance. "You look well."

He stared with grim shock into the laughing brown eyes of his former fiancée. "Giselle. I didn't know you would be here."

"You sent the invitation," she said coyly.

"My mother did. To your family, which included all of its members. I didn't know you were in town."

"Well, here I am." She gave a gay flourish with her satin-gloved hands.

"And your new beau?" he said frostily. "Did he come as well?"

She sighed. "Can we not let bygones be bygones?"

"A flippant reply for one who manipulated my humili-ation in front of the entire town. But what more should I expect? You haven't changed."

Her eyes clouded with what looked like remorse.

"But I have. I'm so very sorry for what I did. I made a mistake, Dalton. I was foolish and selfish."

He didn't deny it.

"I came back to Hillsdale to see you."

He narrowed his eyes in suspicion. "Why?"

"In the hope that you'll let me back into your life."

If Myrna had to hear about another clock, she would smash the next one that gonged the hour. Jeremy had in-troduced her to Franz Schmidt, a clockmaker who boasted of his rare possession of a 17th century cuckoo clock from the Black Forest region of Germany. Her cousin expressed eagerness to see the antique, which led to an invitation to his shop and another rousing conversation of the clock in its years before the pendulum.

Myrna stifled a yawn with her gloved hand and wondered what was so interesting about the workings of a clock. Certainly she was grateful for their ability to display time, but she failed to understand how their housings could lead to such extensive discussions. Clocks were all her cousin talked about—when he wasn't urging her to make a decision.

"I must soon return to my shop," Jeremy stated to Herr Schmidt, capturing Myrna's attention. "I leave on Monday."

She blinked in surprise to hear the news.

"If you're ever in Brighton, you must drop in to see us." To her quiet outrage, Jeremy slipped his hand at the small of her back in a blatant sign of possession. "I have a few collectibles from the former century that might interest you."

Mr. Schmidt toothlessly smiled. "Ja, I should like to see them."

Myrna stared at Jeremy in disbelief, that he would publicly allude to her leaving with him as if it were fact. Her cousin kept his attention focused on the German clockmaker, avoiding her blistering stare. In the company of so many, she could hardly argue the point and excused herself, smiling politely at Herr Schmidt and noting Jeremy's displeased frown now that he did glance her way.

How dare he make such an overt claim on her when he had no right!

Angry fire singed her face. She needed a cool breeze to relieve her senses, and moved through the stifling room and scattered throngs toward the quiet sanctuary of the garden. Off to the side, a couple stood close, near the balustrade, the moment appearing intimate. Recognizing the vibrant woman, Liberty, standing with her sweetheart, two of many guests she'd met within the past hour, Myrna furtively took the path deeper into the garden so as not to disturb the absorbed pair.

Twinges of envy, to know such happiness, made her dwell on her wretched situation while her rapid stride took her farther from the festivities. Soon she became surrounded by tall boxwoods. She wasn't in want of a suitor to marry, but try as she might, she couldn't come up with a plausible excuse to refuse him, save for one.

Her heart belonged to another.

She had not sought it, certainly had not wished for it, had struggled to avoid it—but her feelings had crept up on her, to engulf sound logic and dissolve all reason. Now she was trapped in a bleak situation of her own making that she had no idea how to resolve.

The approach of footsteps had her whirl around, her heart both calming in relief and skipping a beat with nervous anticipation to see his tall figure outlined in the glow of the moon.

"I saw you leave the ballroom," Dalton explained quietly. "You seemed upset."

"I'm fine, thank you." Her steady words belied the fluttering of her pulse.

"It's chilly out here without a wrap. I wouldn't wish you to grow ill."

"I needed some fresh air. I won't stay out long."

He remained immobile. "Are you not enjoying your first ball?"

"It is…an experience. The music is lovely." Strains from the violins drifted to them in the cool night air, even while the silence between them thickened.

"We have not yet had our waltz…"

"What?" she asked in mild alarm as he moved closer.

"…and with our shared distaste for crowded floors, I find this an opportune moment to teach you," he continued as if she'd not spoken.

His hand wrapped softly around her gloved one. Slowly, he pulled her toward him, keeping a decorous amount of space in between, his other hand dropping gently to clasp her waist. His eyes held a shine, though the night stole their color, and Myrna held her breath as he began to move with her along the moonlit path with the lithe elegance she had expected from watching him daily.

The hem of her gown brushed tall hedges as he whirled her about on a walkway designed for two people to stroll side by side. Taken aback by his swift advance, her ability to follow at first came awkward, then more fluid as her body learned the glide of his, and she moved through the simple steps without thought, the night air a silken caress against her skin. She experienced the unladylike urge to press herself against his velvet-trimmed waistcoat, wishing to be wrapped up in his warm strength and forget the rest of the world existed. To forget that demands awaited an answer she dreaded and must soon give. An answer that would dissatisfy one man and shatter her heart that had come so near healing.

Dalton had been nothing but a gentleman, his tender kisses never stolen from her lips but tentatively shared, a silent expression of her hidden attraction to him that only matured with time. As much as she wished to be his, how could she possibly remain at Eagle's Landing?

Is this what happened to her mother? Had that awful man she worked for swept her off her feet and lured her into betrayal, later to bear embittered regrets and a life of ruin? Myrna had suffered fiercely from that scandal and wished it on no one.

And with Dalton, there could be nothing more.

Her cousin was right. A man of his stature would never stoop so low to offer marriage to a simple governess, one soiled by her family's past. Somehow, if she allowed her heart free rein, to do as she wished, he would discover her secret. Just as someone else had not so long ago, destroying what little peace she and Sisi had finally found.

Desperate to escape both Dalton and her punishing thoughts, Myrna moved her fist from clutching her skirts and pressed her palm to his chest. Her fingers trembled to make such bold contact, and she pushed him away.

"Please," she said breathlessly. "No more. I cannot…" The waltz was a custom of the day, a tradition at these extravagant affairs. But to her it had become a moment too bittersweet, his closeness a reminder of what she could never have.

He released her in concern. "Are you all right?"

"My cousin is leaving in two days." She said what she must. "And I've decided to go with him."

Her quiet, cool words fell like shards of ice, slicing through his soul.

"Surely you jest?" Dalton's question came hoarse. "That cannot be your decision."

"It's best for Sisi."

"Notwithstanding the fact that I don't agree with your assessment, have you taken into consideration what that will entail? Chained to a stifling clockmaker's shop, time will become your imprisonment. With nowhere to roam, that is *if you do* have a few minutes to spare for a walk. Cities are crowded and filthy and often rampant with crime."

She blinked at his fierce words. "Jeremy is family. It's what Father would have wanted."

"You hardly know the man!" His heart beat out a staccato of distress at her stubbornness. He had not expected this, had been sure she would stay and come to see Jeremy McBride for the opportunistic wretch that he was.

"Time will change that."

He shook his head. "This isn't like you. The Myrna I met on the train and have come to know would never so meekly enter into a situation that promises more misery than good."

"Perhaps then, you don't know me at all."

Instead of waylaying him, her soft answer propelled Dalton forward. He gripped her upper arms, giving her a little shake and hoping to impart sense.

*"You cannot marry him!"*

It was not fear that sparked in her eyes at his violent whisper but wistfulness, an almost dreamlike quality that made his heart quicken.

"Tell me then, Dalton. Tell me why not?"

The shock of hearing his name spoken so softly on her lips, a first for her and something of which he supposed she wasn't aware, made him wish to draw her into his arms and kiss her senseless. He barely curbed the urge.

"You have a place with us. An excellent position. Rebecca loves you." He let out a breath through clenched teeth and released her in frustration. "It's more than that."

"Yes?" she breathed.

"You're much more than a governess, Myrna. You've become part of this family."

Her eyes clouded, and he wondered if he imagined the change. Did she not wish to have close ties with them?

"I have a family. In Jeremy."

"Jeremy is not your family in any way that counts! You didn't even know of his existence until two years ago." At her surprise, he explained, "He told me. He was quick to fill me in on all the details."

He knew he didn't imagine the alarm that widened her eyes.

"What did he tell you?"

At her fearful whisper, he wondered at the cause. "About the letter your father sent, about how you contacted him after his death."

"Exactly." She seemed to wilt in relief. "I must do this. It's what Father wanted."

"Your father's sole desire was to see that you and your sister were well cared for. You have that here, with us."

"And what of the future?" Her words came leaden. "Rebecca won't always need a governess. I have to consider that, for myself and for my sister. Please respect my decision."

Her skirts brushed him as she walked past. Dalton closed his eyes, feeling as though his heart bled, but did nothing to prevent her retreat.

Once before he had known such helpless anguish. That terrible experience was part of what kept him silent when his mind screamed words he wished to express but could not say. And the stakes were much higher now. No woman had ever captured his heart in such a bewildering manner. From the moment he helped Myrna off the train, she had tested him and tried him and infuriated him—and he'd never felt closer to anyone, never more alive than when in her company.

It wasn't status that kept Dalton silent. He held no shared prejudice or desire to maintain the wretched social standards after all he once suffered at the altar of what was deemed proper. He was a Freed, and in that respect like his father, who did as he pleased, as long as it didn't break moral conventions. The entirety of what restrained Dalton from professing to Myrna the truth of his feelings was what he'd been striving to conquer since his return home. The malady from which she also suffered.

The fear to trust.

He had prayed for wisdom and the ability to break through that wall, and little by little he was accomplishing it. In giving her a chance to prove herself, in accepting her at Eagle's Landing. Later, in offering friendship. A friendship which had blossomed into more on his part... and once again left him in a pit of miserable reflection.

She wished to go. She had made her choice.

Dalton had no hold over her or her heart. And no choice but to stand back and allow her to leave him.

# Chapter 13

Flustered by her encounter with Dalton, Myrna thought about leaving the ball and taking refuge in her room. Yet it would be rude to disappear, and she did not wish to offend her hostess. She couldn't speak to his mother, not yet, not after what had just occurred, and spotting an empty seat by the wall next to a young woman intently watching the festivities, she moved toward it.

"Do you mind?" Myrna asked, motioning to the chair.

The woman smiled. "Not at all. The seat's not taken. I'm Olive Wittingham."

"Myrna McBride." She gave a polite smile in return, hoping her face had cooled to a normal shade of pale and sat beside her.

"You're new to Hillsdale, aren't you? I don't believe we've met."

"I came by accident," Myrna quipped. "I was on one of the trains that collided in February," she explained upon seeing Olive's blank stare. "I work for the Freeds."

"Really? My mother was a maid here some time ago, for Dalton's father and Mrs. Freed. After she married, he would visit my father's shop. They became friends. My parents have long since passed away, but the Freeds still reach out in friendship and invite me to the ball every year." She giggled. "I shouldn't even be here. I'm a hotel laundress, certainly not one of the upper or even middle crust who comes to these events."

Myrna nodded in understanding. "Neither should I. I'm the governess."

"Yet here we are." A twinkle lit Olive's eyes. "Two peas in a pod in a room full of glazed ducklings."

The bizarre analogy made Myrna laugh, though her heart twisted at how apt and far-reaching the differences truly were.

A sour expression crossed the woman's face as if she'd bit into a lemon, and Myrna looked toward the dance floor to see what upset her. The musicians had shifted to another song and the guests were lined up in two rows facing each other, performing a series of complicated steps while holding their hands up and walking slowly around their partner, also taking turns with others dancers. She inhaled a breath to see Dalton dancing with a beautiful brunette. He looked beyond the woman, never meeting her eyes, his expression stiff, but she smiled up at him while she spoke, seeming happy to be near him.

Myrna couldn't help feel a little stab of jealousy.

"I cannot believe she had the audacity to show her face here," Olive said in disgust, "but what is he doing even *dancing* with her? He should have thrown her out the door!"

Myrna saw that Olive was also staring at Dalton and the woman.

"Who is she?"

"Giselle Dubois. The hussy who returned to Hillsdale."

Myrna looked at Olive, surprised by her low, vehement words.

"I'm sorry." Olive looked penitent. "That wasn't very charitable of me. But it made me so angry when she left Dalton at the altar."

"Left Dalton at the altar?" Myrna repeated dumbly.

"That's actually a poor choice of words since she never showed up. The poor man, and the church packed to the gills, too! Reverend Scott was so kind—" she said, her cheeks going rosy at mention of the pastor "—taking him aside, giving him her letter. It crushed Dalton to learn that the faithless hussy had run off with another man. Good riddance, I say."

Myrna felt stunned to realize that her previous assumption of Dalton's character had been incorrect. He had *not* been to blame for the scandal. She looked back to the floor. Dalton still seemed tense, but he no longer avoided Giselle and now spoke to her. She no longer smiled, but stared up at him intently.

"Dalton left Hillsdale that week," Olive continued, "went to New York to attend university. His father's alma mater. Didn't expect him home so soon. He must have been there only one term, but with his brother's death, I suppose he had no choice. I hope he has the good sense not to fall into her clutches a second time."

Myrna barely heard what Olive said. Her somber gaze remained fixed on the couple. She had unjustly thought him a cad and now felt remorseful for her unsavory opinion of his character, however defensive her reasoning had been. Her relief to see them change partners as the dance progressed was short-lived. Once the song ended Giselle again approached him, linking her arm with his and steering him toward the foyer.

Myrna swallowed over the painful lump in her throat. She had no cause to feel hurt. She had informed him of her decision to marry another man. She would be leaving in two days. If he wished to rekindle an old romance, no matter how unwise, that wasn't her concern.

The logical assertions rang hollow in her mind, the music that surrounded her blithe and gay in its mockery.

She *was* hurt, and what was worse, she couldn't do a blessed thing about it. She had done this, in allowing herself to do what she swore she never would.

She had fallen in love with Dalton Freed.

It was with an almost tearful rush of relief that she noticed her cousin standing off to the side, near the hearth, alone. Another ordinary pea in her common pod. She made her excuses to Olive and moved to join him, for the first time almost eager to hear about his clocks. Almost...

At present, she welcomed anything to drown out the silent weeping of her soul.


"Tell me, honestly, what do you hope to gain?"

Dalton wearied of Giselle's relentless flirtation and said what needed to be said. They had the foyer to themselves, the doors to the ballroom closed and muffling the music within. He had been dismayed to find her as one of his partners in the ever-shifting quadrille and had woodenly gone through the steps, not wishing to cause a scene by leaving in the middle of the dance.

Of course, she had followed.

"Always so candid," she teased, hitting his arm with her fan. "You were like that when we were children, too."

"This isn't a game, Giselle."

"Your faith teaches forgiveness." She pouted. "Why can you not forgive?"

"It was difficult, but I have forgiven you," he admitted, and she smiled. "But that isn't the same as accepting you back into my life."

A hard glint lit her dark eyes. "Have you met someone else, then?"

He thought of Myrna and her beautiful evergreen eyes that were so sincere, even when in her fright she once tried to deceive. The memory made him wish to find her and draw her into his arms, to plead with her to stay and vow to protect her from whatever evil still threatened. He had long sensed that she feared something or someone from her past, but she would never play a man's heart like a toy, to be tossed aside when it lost its appeal.

"Why did you leave Jason?" he asked.

"Jason is a child. He squandered away his inheritance in under four months. Can you believe it?"

"Yes, frankly, I can." He regarded her grimly. "So you've come back, hoping for a slice of the Freed wealth?"

She gasped. "That was cruel."

"It was honest."

"You make me sound like a gold digger."

"What am I supposed to think? Perhaps if you really wish for a place in my life again, you should become Rebecca's governess. Our current governess is leaving in two days to live with a cousin." He said the harsh words in jest. Never would he allow Giselle to raise his niece and never would Giselle agree, her fondness for children mild in the extreme. Another area where they differed. He wanted a house full of them.

A stir at the upper landing had him lift his head to see a blur of nightgowns and small bare feet running toward the corridor.

"I'm not without means." Giselle's hurt words brought his attention back to her. "Or have you forgotten that my father is well-to-do in his own right?" Her dark eyes were wounded. "When we were young, we were such good friends—and now you hate me?"

He sighed. "I don't hate you." He realized it was true.

For a short time after his public humiliation, he did. Now he felt…nothing, even surprised that he once felt something. Their long association had led him to believe friendship was love. But he realized the strength of what he felt for Myrna in a matter of months, a need which burned through his heart in its intensity, did not compare to the weaker affection he once felt for Giselle.

"I don't hate you," he repeated softly. "But since we're speaking of it, tell me. I must know. Why did you not tell me of your strong affection for Jason *before* the day we were to be wed? You never before acted so harshly toward me. I had no warning, none whatsoever."

Tears glimmered in her eyes. "I didn't love Jason," she whispered, and he sensed this was no act. Her facade seemed to crumble.

"Then why…?"

"Oh, Dalton." She shook her head. "Your family is so perfect. *You're* perfect. I couldn't begin to compare—the Freeds are a paragon of virtue and importance in this town. I was terrified that one day you would come to realize I didn't fit in and see me for who I am. I left before you could hurt me."

"You thought so little of me?"

Sudden insight came to him as he recalled her father's philandering ways.

"I am by no means perfect, Giselle, but I would have been faithful to you."

"I know." The tears trembled on her lashes and he reached for his handkerchief, handing it to her. "But it's always been said that I'm my father's daughter, and he can be heartless. As you know, I was his biggest disappointment, ever since he discovered he had a daughter and not a son. But I want you to know—" she wrung his handkerchief in her hands "—I was never *with* Jason. He was just…a shared adventure. I suppose that in my recklessness I threw away whatever reputation I had, and that was foolish. But *that's* who I am, Dalton. I don't think before I act. I never have, and I don't know how to be different."

He had not felt such closeness with her in years as he felt in that moment, but it was an intimacy borne of old camaraderie. Gone were the feckless pretensions and dogged flirtations that had become her trade. The open expression of the woman before him reminded Dalton of the shy girl who, one frozen winter's day, asked if he would carry her books since she'd left her mittens behind and needed to warm her hands in her coat. He had lent her his oversize gloves and carried her books, and that blustery walk to school had been the start of a friendship that in their adulthood they tried to make into more, as was expected in their circle....

Even when more didn't fit.

He realized that he'd been as much to blame for what went wrong between them.

"We're both guilty of being rash at times, when we want something badly enough." He kept his voice low in reassurance, taking the handkerchief from her tense hands and gently dabbing at her tears. "The truth is, you ran away, Giselle, because you *didn't want* the life I would have given you. And if you're honest with yourself, that hasn't changed. Some friendships are meant to stay that way."

Quiet acceptance came into her eyes. "You're right. I guess that's part of why I left. I knew I could never be the wife you deserved. It wasn't in me." She broke off and shook her head. "I still care about you, Dalton. I always will."

"I know." He pressed his lips to her forehead in a tender seal of forgiveness then stepped back. "As will I."

She tried to smile and laughed aloud in a half sob of

self-derision. "I came here tonight with every intention of winning you back...."

"And in the process, rediscovered a friend," he added quietly when her soft words trailed away.

# Chapter 14

Myrna entered the conservatory, the beautiful music easing her troubled mind. She stood for a moment, surprised to see Dalton at the piano. She hadn't thought to find him here alone.

Her courage floundered. She moved to retreat when his nimble hands on the keys stopped. He turned as if sensing her presence.

"Myrna?"

She inwardly scowled at the foolish rush of pleasure caused from hearing him say her name.

"I wanted to speak with you...."

She approached and he stood to his feet in question.

"Sisi and I will be leaving in the morning."

His eyes grew distant. "Then I wish you all the best. I won't be here when you go. I'm meeting with the new manager I hired to take over the mill. I'm working to bring about the reforms you and I spoke of."

At the solemn manner in which he said the last, as if her

opinion truly mattered, she swallowed hard. "I'm pleased to hear it. Um, Jeremy mentioned that your pocket watch is broken?"

At the waver in her voice and complete change of topic, he looked at her oddly but nodded. "I had hoped he might fix it or tell me it was salvageable, but unfortunately it isn't."

She pulled the gold disc from her skirt pocket and handed it to him. "I want you to have this. It was my father's," she explained, putting the treasured pocket watch into his hand, the chain trickling and looping over his fingers.

He looked at her in shock. "You're giving me your father's watch?"

His words grew even softer in disbelief, and she blinked hard.

"Yes. I—I want you to have it. It's probably not as nice as the one you had, but it works. You've been so kind, and I wanted to give you something—"

He grasped her arms, stunning her into silence, the chain dangling from his hand.

"Don't go." The harsh plea in his voice matched the desperation in his eyes, and her heart echoed his low cry. "Please, Myrna, I couldn't bear it."

"I have no choice," she whispered.

"What do you mean? *Of course* you have a choice!"

She shook her head, wishing she hadn't let that slip.

His jaw went hard. "Is your cousin threatening you?"

"No, it's nothing like that."

"Then *what* is it? You cannot leave us, Myrna, leave me. Surely you must know how I've come to feel about you?"

She did, and that scared her the most since she returned his feelings. But she would not give in to temptation and be like her mother, would not give in to a life of sin to be with this man....

"I had not allowed myself to hope, not until now, but with your sweet gift—you must feel some affection for me?" His words were persuasion-laced in vulnerability, and she couldn't prevent the little nod and rush of tears that followed.

"Yes."

At her meek answer he heavily exhaled as if he'd been holding his breath.

"Dearest Myrna, you are like sunshine warming my soul that's been too long frozen. I need you to stay here, with me." His words were a bare whisper, and when he lifted his hands to cradle her face, she didn't pull away.

His mouth pressed flush to hers, nothing like before, this kiss deep and warming her, making her wish to draw him still closer. "Please, don't," she breathed without sincerity as she faintly turned her head away, her hands still clutching his waistcoat.

"What are you afraid of?" He pressed his forehead to her temple, his hands moving down to grip her waist. "I'd never hurt you. Don't you know that?"

His tender words floated to the hollow chamber of her heart. Oh, how she longed to believe him! Drawn to the need for his touch, wishing for his embrace, she turned her mouth back to his, again allowing him to drink from her lips, before harsh reality again interfered.

"No!" Trembling, she stepped back, into the curve of the grand piano. "I'm to marry Jeremy."

"You can't!" His words were low and fierce. "Not with the way we feel about each other. Not now that we've both *admitted it!*"

She shook her head tearfully. "But what is there for us?"

He looked so distraught that his pain wrenched her heart. All she wanted was to assure him of her love and be reassured of his.

She barely held back from initiating another kiss.

He opened his mouth to speak.

The door opened and Rebecca walked inside. Her eyes widened upon seeing Dalton and Myrna standing close, with his hands at her waist. Quickly he dropped them to his sides and stepped back while Myrna lowered her palms from his chest and moved away from the piano. She struggled with embarrassment to be caught in such an intimate moment.

"Rebecca." She cleared the huskiness from her throat. "Is there something you wanted?"

"I was looking for Nana."

"She's upstairs resting." Dalton's voice came low.

Myrna looked toward the door, glad her sister had not seen them.

"Is Sisi not with you?"

Rebecca glanced at the carpet. "No."

"Do you know where she is?"

Rebecca shrugged. "In her room?"

Myrna hadn't seen her sister since that morning, but with Sisi's latest penchant for hiding, sometimes even making it into a game, Myrna wasn't overly concerned.

"I should go talk to her." She still hadn't told Sisi they were leaving, wishing to put off the difficult moment as long as possible. But it was now time she be told.

Myrna shared a look with Dalton. His eyes were sad, silently begging her to stay. She wished that he would speak, to end what she'd put in motion, but knew it was futile to hope for such words from him. With nothing more to say, she offered a trembling smile of farewell and left him standing there.

As she ascended the staircase, the tears clouding her eyes, her thoughts went to the well-read novel sitting by her bedside, and again she noted similarities to her wretched life. Mr. Rochester had been stubborn, even cruel, but Jane endured, until the moment everything changed and she thought happiness could be hers. At the peak of discovery, that joy, too, had been ripped from her, and she escaped to survive. As Myrna must do, as she always had done, in trying to carve out what satisfactory life she could glean from this mortal existence.

*Dear God, help me to endure this!*

With a little shock, she became aware that she had reached out to the Almighty in her pain. What's more, she felt an odd glimmer of hope, unfamiliar to her, that He might truly be listening.

Dalton watched Myrna go, heaviness settling in his chest as he sank to the bench.

He had not expounded on the depth of his feelings, had not thought at all beyond his objective to make Myrna see that her place was with them at Eagle's Landing, *with him.* He could plainly see that she was entering into a choice she had no desire to make. The forlorn look in her eyes spoke more eloquently than her words of duty, which rang hollow and without substance.

So why in blazes was she doing this?

His laugh came without amusement upon realizing he had acted with the same impulsiveness that less than twenty-four hours ago he assured Giselle both were capable of. At least some good had come from the debacle they created, the walls of artifice finally destroyed. They might never regain their friendship to the degree it was, but the angry bitterness had dissolved. Now the only emotion left was the empty ache inside his heart at losing Myrna.

Perhaps he shouldn't have kissed her. But she had kissed him back, so she must feel something. Or was he seeing only what he wished to? Had Dalton been forcing his affections on her rather than attempting to bring her to the knowledge of her feelings for him? The possibility stung.

Maybe she truly did wish to go with her cousin. Other than Sisi, Jeremy was the only family she had left.

But the gift of the pocket watch told him a different story, as had the windows of her eyes when she'd put it into his hand, and he looked at the treasured item he still held by its chain. It was of value in more ways than worth. Instead of giving it to the man who made his living with timepieces and would consider it an honor to receive the family heirloom, she'd given it to Dalton, who considered it no less an honor. He brushed his thumb over the engraved disc, flipped it open, and faintly smiled to see its working face.

The door burst open. He shot to his feet as Myrna hurried inside.

"I cannot find Sisi!" She released the words in a rush of panic. "Rebecca doesn't know where she is. No one does."

He covered the distance and clasped her shoulders in reassurance. "She's done this before, yes?" He kept his tone light. "We'll find her."

She nodded, her eyes no less worried but now hopeful.

They left the conservatory. Finding Genevieve in the corridor, he instructed, "Spread the word to the servants to search the house for Sisi. Tell Jonas and Charles to search the grounds and stables."

"Aye, Mr. Freed."

She hurried off and Dalton swiftly continued to the library, Myrna beside him. They encountered her cousin along the way.

"Sisi is missing," Myrna greeted.

Jeremy frowned. "She's only being defiant. She'll turn up soon."

"I feel it's more. Could she have learned we were leaving? Did you tell her?"

Dalton directed a sharp glance her way as a memory returned. "The girls were eavesdropping on the party. They might have heard me speak to Giselle. I told her of your plans to leave."

He wondered if he imagined the flash of jealous hurt in her eyes at mention of his ex-fiancée.

"That must be it, then," Myrna said. "She's hiding."

"I hope the girl isn't always this much trouble," Jeremy grumbled as they continued down the corridor. "Can't have her disturbing customers in my shop with her silly games."

Myrna frowned. "Exactly what will Sisi do there?"

"Don't trust children around my clocks. Children break things. She'll stay above in the room, where we'll live."

"And what of her education?"

"You can teach her if you like. Isn't that what you've been doing?"

"What about fresh air?" Myrna insisted. "A place for her to play?"

"You lived in the city. You know how it is. In the business district where I live, the streets are narrow, the buildings close, but she'll make do, as other children have."

Dalton barely refrained from replying, disgusted to hear of such an undesirable future mapped out for the child. Myrna took a stand against bad conditions for the workers in factories and mills. Could she not see that the future described for her little sister held bleak similarities?

An hour of searching produced no sign of the girl. Worry escalated into fear as Myrna clutched Dalton's sleeve like a lifeline. Jeremy had long ago quit the search, with the excuse that they had plenty of help, would find her soon enough, and he and Myrna had an early train to catch, adding that he certainly had no time to pander to Sisi's nonsense.

"Rebecca," Dalton said to his niece as he caught sight of her in the moment she made as if to hurry away upon noticing them.

"Yes, Uncle Dalton?"

He wasn't tricked by her apparent cooperation and regarded her sternly. "If you know anything about Sisi's disappearance you must tell me."

She pouted. "She doesn't want to go, and I don't want her to. She's my friend."

Dalton shared a look of relief with Myrna then again turned his attention to his errant niece. "Did you hide her like last time?" When she stubbornly pressed her lips together, he insisted, "Answer me!"

"You'll make her go away on the train." Rebecca's lip trembled. "She hates trains. She's scared of them."

Myrna bent down to her level. "I love Sisi and only want what's best for her. Please, Rebecca, tell me where she is. I've been so worried."

"Rebecca…"

Dalton's warning tone served to deflate the girl's bravado. "You weren't supposed to know she was gone till tomorrow, after the train went away. And then you would stay. Like last time."

"Where is she?" Dalton's tone lost its tension but remained firm.

"In the locked room." Rebecca pulled a key from her dress and handed it to him.

"You locked her in the old playroom?"

Rebecca nodded.

Dalton felt a chill brush over his soul. He hurried to the third floor, Myrna and Rebecca in his wake.

Upon unlocking and opening the door, he found the playroom empty.

"Sisi?" Myrna called but received no reply.

Dalton's gaze flew to the window, his actions taking him there as with trembling hands he pulled back the heavy drape. The pane was locked.

"Where is she?" he asked Rebecca.

"I don't know," she said, looking as puzzled as he felt.

Dalton scanned the room, his attention falling on the old wardrobe against the wall. His heart lurched in dread.

"Sisi," he called, hurrying to the huge article of furniture. He tried the door. It wouldn't budge. The tricky latch had again slipped as had often been the case when he was a boy. Looking around the room, he motioned to a heavy block of wood carved into a toy wagon that sat near Myrna.

"Give me that."

With wide eyes, she did as ordered. He struck the handle with the wood three times, at last breaking through. The door swung open. Myrna gasped in horror, and dread clutched Dalton's heart at the sight of the wan child lying insensible and half-hidden in a pile of old coats.

Carefully, much as he had done on the train months before, he pulled Sisi from her hiding place. She did not stir. Her face felt clammy, her hair damp and clinging to her perspiring skin. To his relief, she still breathed, but it came reedy and faint.

"Is she all right?" Rebecca asked, her voice wobbly with fear. "Why won't she wake up?"

Myrna's terrified eyes asked the same question.

He wished he could again offer reassurance but felt none to give. Rising to his feet, he held the limp child carefully in his arms. "We must send Jonas for the doctor."

## Chapter 15

The next hours were a blur for Myrna. Once Dalton carried Sisi to her bedroom, they were able to revive her with a wet cloth, but she still lay so very weak, and her heartfelt whisper, "Please don't make me go," tore at Myrna's heart. Within the hour the doctor arrived, his prognosis not severe but not inspiring. After Myrna answered questions with regard to Sisi's medical history, he grimly ordered that the girl have complete bed rest the following day and to send for him if her condition worsened.

Myrna had never drawn closer to the Lord as she did that night, while sitting by her sister's bedside and holding her limp hand as Sisi lay in deep slumber. Her faith had broadened to reach out for Divine guidance, but her shame intensified to acknowledge her ineptitude.

Hearing a step on the threshold, she turned to look.

"I did this to her," she whispered, guilt ready to consume her.

Dalton approached and crouched beside her chair,

clutching one arm of it. "You can't think like that. You're not to blame."

"Who else?" Tears trembled at the edges of her lashes and slid down her cheeks as she closed her eyes. "She fears trains so much, but I wouldn't listen. Thinking she would get over it. Thinking I knew what was best. Thinking I could always keep her safe. She almost suffocated because of me! I *almost killed* my baby sister." She let out a soft, strangled sob. "And she's not out of the woods yet. She's never been strong, we almost lost her as a babe. She always succumbed to illnesses first, taking the longest to recover—"

Myrna's words came to an abrupt halt at the warm brush of Dalton's thumb against her cheek, wiping away her tears, his fingertips lightly resting against her ear. She opened her eyes to look at him.

"May I tell you a story?" he asked, gentleness and sorrow softening his expression.

She nodded.

With no other chair in the room, he moved to sit on the floor, his back against the bed, the soles of his shoes planted on the rug. He clasped one hand around his wrist tightly, placing them atop his bent knees.

"I've told you about Alyssa," he began, "but I never spoke of the day she died. I was nine. She was seven."

Myrna held her breath, afraid to say a word, afraid that he wouldn't continue if she did. She had long wondered about what happened but never wished to stir up old pain.

"We were much closer in age than Roger and I, and Alyssa followed me everywhere. Like a shadow." A sad smile touched his lips. "Sometimes I didn't mind, we were playmates, but as I grew older, I desired time to myself. In the locked playroom, there's a window…" His eyes fell shut as if unable to face what came next. "I was like every boy, full of adventure. That day, I decided it would be exciting to walk across the narrow ledge that borders that side of the manor to the turret window. Several steps across, I heard a noise and looked over my shoulder. Alyssa was on the ledge."

Fresh tears stung Myrna's eyes as she suddenly knew what he would say.

"I remember as if it were yesterday. I ordered her back to the playroom, saying that little girls shouldn't climb high places, and continued walking. She insisted that if I could do it, so could she. I told her if she didn't stop following me I would jump off the edge and fly away. She insisted she would do the same and I couldn't get rid of her. I argued that I could and was about to tell her that girls couldn't fly, that I was a pirate walking a plank and she couldn't be one, too, when I heard it. The most awful sound, I'll never forget it. Her gasp, the rustle of cloth, a yelp of fear—then nothing. I swung my head around to look, but she wasn't there. Then I saw her. Below. Lying so still in the grass, like a broken doll..."

His cheeks glistened with tears. Unable to refrain, Myrna reached out and brushed them away, as he'd done for her. Without opening his eyes, he grabbed her hand and pressed her fingertips to his lips hard. She inhaled a soft breath at the little shock of warmth that rushed through her at his unexpected act.

"I'm not sure how I got off that ledge without also falling. I don't remember much that happened afterward, I think I must have been in a state of shock. Mother never audibly blamed me, but she's not forgotten. I sometimes still hear her rocking in the playroom late in the night. The chair creaks and makes the sound of a weeping child, covering any sound as she also weeps. She thinks I don't know. Alyssa's death caused a rift between my parents that took a long time to heal. Father remained cold toward me, and that's why I believe he never taught me the family business. I wasn't a worthy son. Alyssa was always his favorite."

"Dalton, you're not to blame for what happened," Myrna hastened to assure, hearing the self-censure in his tone.

He looked at her then, his eyes steady. "No more than you are to blame for what happened to Sisi."

She drew a harsh breath, understanding why he'd chosen this moment to confide in her.

"That's different. I'm a grown woman. You were a child."

"We all make mistakes based on bad choices we think are suitable at the time. I no longer blame myself, though the memory of that day is still difficult to face, like Sisi fears trains and hides herself away from the prospect of boarding one. My mother put the lock on the playroom door for *my benefit*. But a time comes when locks need to be broken. When the past can suffocate the present and make it hard, if not impossible to move on."

His quiet words reached deep into Myrna's soul, shaking the foundation of all she'd been taught to survive. She had secured her own locks to hide away from all that her family had suffered. Perhaps it was the lateness of the hour, the atmosphere conducive to intimacy and baring secrets... perhaps it was the trust that Dalton placed in her by speaking of his troubled past, which she felt certain was rare...

But suddenly she wanted him to know the truth.

She glanced at the bed to make sure that Sisi was still sound asleep. "When I was very young," she said above a whisper, a slight waver giving away her nervousness, "after my father had the accident and could no longer find work, my mother secured a position as companion to a wealthy but demanding woman she had known since childhood. I told you that weeks ago." She often had wondered if the dowager's son had orchestrated the arrangement.

He nodded, and with shame she briefly told of her mother's indiscretions, and how Sisi was the product of them. She spoke of how scandal visited the family, how she'd seen the illicit kiss, how her father had awakened her late one night, after having been accused of stealing an heirloom piece of the dowager's jewelry—though to this day Myrna felt that her principled father had been set up by the dowager's son—and how they fled into a life of near poverty. She tensed as she came to her part of the story and realized with some surprise that despite her tainted confession, he had not let go of her hand. The knowledge gave her the courage to continue and face her own monsters.

"After Father died I was excited to find work at the new library. My love of literature made me a worthy aide, and I was content there for months. Then an older gentleman entered one afternoon and visited every day for a week— Mr. Parker, a wealthy, influential merchant who I learned had lived in the town where I grew up. He recognized me, since I favor my mother. He was kind the first several days, drawing me into conversations with him, and I thought him a gentleman. Then one evening he cornered me while I was shelving books." Her face burned with embarrassment to whisper the next words. "He wanted me to—to be his mistress. He told me he would make my life one of ease, that I never had to work another day, but I refused. He threatened that if I didn't comply he would tell my manager of the old scandal, of my mother's sins and my father's alleged theft. I begged him not to speak of it, but he refused to listen. He gave me one day to decide then left, but of course I could never do such a thing. So he did as he'd warned, also lying that I was a thief, and I was discharged.

"Later, he approached me again, thinking that with no income I would become agreeable to his proposition, and offered to set me up in an apartment. No matter how much I refused, he wouldn't leave me be, and I feared that one day he wouldn't take no for an answer. So I took Sisi and fled to another town. I found work sewing. Later, a job as a laundress. When Sisi grew ill, I stayed home to take care of her and lost that position, too. That's when I wrote my cousin. I pawned Mother's jewelry to cover my debts and the train tickets—except for this. And I kept Papa's watch."

She fingered the wedding ring she still wore, for no other purpose except she had no place safe to put it. Her venture into trust had not yet extended to the household staff, to leave it just sitting out in her bedchamber.

"That explains so much," he said quietly.

Throughout the grim recounting she had kept her eyes on her sister but now looked at him.

"Meaning?"

"Your behavior when you first arrived. Why you didn't wish to come home with me, when I first found you."

He made it sound intimate, and she lowered her gaze, her cheeks warming.

"Myrna, as I've said many times, I would never harm you. Please tell me you believe that now."

She nodded without hesitation.

"And I'm sorry if I only added to your difficult circumstances."

She looked at him in confusion.

"My behavior in the conservatory," he clarified. "I shouldn't have forced my attentions on you, giving you further cause for distress. I should have honored your decision. My actions were reprehensible."

Disappointment that he apologized for a token of affection that meant a great deal to her made it difficult to reply. "You've done nothing worthy of forgiveness. I didn't exactly pull away."

His eyes flicked up to hers, alert.

Realizing that once again she had revealed too much, she felt a new flush of warmth.

"Myrna…"

"Uncle Dalton?"

At the sound of Rebecca's voice, both of them swung their attention to the entrance. His niece stood there in her long ruffled bed gown, fear inscribed on every feature.

"Is she going to die?" Rebecca whispered, her voice trembling, and Myrna flinched at the words. "We weren't trying to be naughty. We wanted to save her from the wolf, like the huntsman saved Little Red Cap."

*The wolf?*

Myrna recalled her little sister's remarks the day of their cousin's arrival.

Of course. Jeremy.

"I didn't know she'd crawl into the cupboard. I didn't know it would get stuck."

At the almost hysterical hitch in her voice, Dalton rose from the floor. "One moment," he said to Myrna, then approached his niece, putting his hand to her shoulder and steering her away. "Come, Rebecca. We must talk."

Myrna stared after them, curious what he would tell the child but mostly wondering what he had been about to say.

"Uncle Dalton, you don't like him, either. I can tell."

His niece climbed into bed, and Dalton pulled the sheet over her, to her chin.

"Regardless of my feelings for Miss McBride's cousin, it was wrong of you to interfere."

He was resigned to let Myrna go, no matter how hollow he felt at the prospect. Distancing himself from the manor at dawn and not returning until after she left would be the wisest recourse to carry out the difficult choice.

"Promise Sisi won't die?"

His rigid stance softened at her plea, and he sat down on the edge of her bed, taking her small hand in his.

"I'm not God. I can't make such promises. No one can.

But remember what Nana says, how we must have faith and not waver in the midst of any storm. You must pray and hold on to faith that God always does what is best, as tightly as I'm holding to your hand."

"Like the eagle who won't give up?" she asked quietly. "Like our family creed?"

"Exactly."

She looked at him with childlike trust then smiled. "You called her Myrna."

"What?" Taken aback, he tried to keep up with his niece's wandering mind.

"I heard you at the door. And you hugged her in the conservatory. You *like* her."

Dalton released her hand. "To bed, Rebecca. We'll discuss suitable discipline for your misbehavior tomorrow when I return from town."

She wrinkled her nose then smiled again. "I think she likes you, too."

Dalton renounced the leap his heart made at such naïve words and tweaked her nose. "You're incorrigible."

She giggled then grew serious. "She cries sometimes while we're doing lessons. She goes and looks out the window and cries so we can't hear. She always brushes her cheeks before she turns around."

Such news wounded Dalton to hear it, sure he must have been partly responsible for Myrna's sorrow, and his resolve strengthened. He would not be the source of her tears again.

"You shouldn't tell me such things."

"She doesn't want to go away, so why is she leaving?" Rebecca insisted.

A question he asked himself more than once. He stood and lowered the lamp to a dull flame. "Good night, Rebecca."

He was halfway to the door when she again spoke.

"I know Sisi is going to be all right, 'cause I'm going to pray really hard and have faith."

He turned at the threshold. "That's my girl. Now go to sleep."

Obediently she closed her eyes. "And I'm going to pray that Miss Myrna stays with us."

In the lamp's gentle glow a peaceful expression soon calmed her face. For Dalton, with all he had learned and revealed tonight, he felt certain that slumber would not be so benevolent toward him.

## Chapter 16

Dawn broke through the crack in the panes, bathing that sliver of the room in muted rose, and startled by the light Myrna jerked awake in the chair, her first realization—Dalton had gone.

Last night he had returned to keep vigil with her, bringing with him two tankards of coffee. But any deep revelations did not resume as within minutes of his arrival, Sisi awakened from a nightmare. Terrified, she had clasped both Myrna's hand and Dalton's, saying she felt safer with "Uncle Dalton" and Myrna both there. Dalton stayed long after he told her a story to help her sleep, not of wolves or other terrors, but this one of a princess and a pea that made Sisi drowsily smile. The remaining hours he encouraged Myrna and told tales of his past with his siblings, and she also recounted some of the happier events of her childhood.

Genevieve entered the room, clearly surprised to see Myrna there.

"Go," she encouraged. "Get some rest. I'll stay with the wee one."

With a glance at Sisi to assure she slept peacefully, Myrna thanked the maid and went to her room. She sluiced her face with cool water from the washstand, changed into a fresh dress, then wearily made her way downstairs to find sustenance.

Jeremy met her in the foyer.

"Glad to see you're up and about," he greeted her and checked his pocket watch. "We haven't much time before the train leaves."

"I'm sorry. I cannot possibly leave today."

He frowned. "I've spent too much time away from my shop. My assistant sent a telegram that one of my most valued clients needs help, which he isn't qualified to give."

She took the remaining steps down. "You had already retired for the night. You didn't know. We found Sisi—"

He gave an impatient nod. "A maid told me. Are your bags packed?"

"A doctor had to be sent for. He said she's to remain the day in bed."

"She'll be fine once we're aboard the train."

"No, you don't understand. She…she could have died last night, smothered to death."

It still hurt saying it.

A trace of sympathy touched his eyes. "But she's all right now?"

"I wouldn't say that, but she's better."

He shrugged. "Then I don't see the problem."

Myrna struggled to remain composed in the face of his cavalier attitude toward her little sister.

"*The problem* is that due to her history of illness I would prefer to follow the doctor's orders."

He thought it over then gave a short nod. "I'm not a

cruel man, Myrna. If she needs to stay, so be it. We can send for her later."

"Send for her?"

"Yes. Now what's the matter? I thought that would please you."

"I can't send Sisi alone on a train—she fears the very thought of them! I would need to accompany her."

"You mollycoddle the girl, Myrna." Anger laced his words and he snapped his pocket watch shut. "My father would never have allowed what she gets away with on a daily basis. She must learn her place."

Myrna struggled to keep the ice from freezing her tone. "And just what is *her place?*"

"Seen, not heard, as all children should be. Definitely not having every whim catered to. She needs a firm hand. Then, once she's of age, she might make a suitable match for my apprentice."

"You're joking."

"Don't look so shocked. Arranged marriages happen all the time. He's a fine boy, highly skilled, and I wouldn't wish to lose him."

Barely seven, and he was marrying her sister off for his convenience?

The truth came to Myrna so vividly, it brought a rush of relief, like lancing a boil, though she was sure Jeremy would protest to being compared to a carbuncle. She almost felt giddy with contained laughter at the parallel, or perhaps it was due to her lack of sleep.

"I'm sorry. This was a mistake."

"What was?"

"I cannot leave with you."

The soft words aired gave her solid conviction and she faintly smiled.

His face reddened. He looked ready to explode and

pocketed his watch. "Fine. If it's that important, stay and travel with your sister later. I must leave today."

Before he took more than a few steps toward the staircase, she stopped him with her next words.

"You misunderstood. I cannot go at all. I cannot marry you."

He gaped at her in shock.

"I'm sorry it's taken me this long to realize. So many fears clouded my perception. But the life you offer isn't what I want for my sister. It isn't the life I would choose for myself."

"You're not thinking clearly." His tone was condescending. "You look like you've had no sleep. Don't make rash decisions you'll later regret."

"Actually, I'm thinking more clearly than I have in a long while. I would make a terrible clockmaker's wife. I find the topic of clocks rather dull and certainly wouldn't wish to spend the remainder of my days dusting them."

He stared at her, as if more horrified by that disclosure than by her change of heart. She wondered what he would say if she admitted that she found him to be of similar character to his clocks but refrained from speaking the insult. He had been kind to respond to her letter and follow her father's wish to help. Myrna had no desire to rub salt in the wound.

"Goodbye, Jeremy. I do wish you the very best life has to offer," she said, sincerely meaning it, "and a pleasant journey home."

"But—what will you do?" he asked once Myrna walked away.

She turned slightly to look at him. "I haven't decided. But I'm no longer apprehensive of what the future might bring."

He gave her a nod of grudging acknowledgment, and she wondered if secretly he was relieved, having also come to the conclusion that she and Sisi wouldn't fit into his rigid lifestyle that ran like his mechanical clocks.

Needing fresh air and open space, she went outdoors.

Dalton's surprising acceptance of her, after hearing of her family's scandal, had been a huge burden lifted from her shoulders. He and his mother had been the two she most feared would want nothing more to do with her if her history came to light. Instead, Dalton had opened up to her, and she felt twice ashamed for misjudging him.

But that didn't change their lots in life or erase the feelings experienced when in his presence, when in his arms. Friendship and desire were not love. She had grown to treasure his companionship, but knew it would never be enough. For either of them.

She trusted Dalton never to wield his position to try to seek more from her but didn't place faith in herself, not after her passionate reaction to his embraces. She had never felt that way with any man before Dalton, and she had no wish to tempt fate, to learn if she was as weak as her mother. Perhaps the girl Olive might speak for her to her manager, and Myrna could secure a position as a laundress, also find a place in town for her and Sisi to board.

Without realizing she'd done so, Myrna found herself on the plot of land that held the family tombstones. Twice in the span of months death tried to steal her sister, and she could not help but thank God that He watched out for them. How much she had changed from the suspicious and terrified woman Dalton first brought to this house against her will!

With tears in her eyes, she smiled at the memory and looked at Dalton's brother's grave. His death was the reason Dalton returned home, and though the events were tragic, she felt blessed to have been a passenger on the train with him. Where would she be now if they had never crossed paths? So much had happened since that night to change her outlook on life. She felt that she had aged years instead of months.

She stared at the small, gray headstone in the row behind, with an angel carved into its stone surface. It was clear that Dalton loved his little sister and still carried guilty remorse for her death, though he, too, had learned to move on, as difficult as that could be.

The sudden blur of movement in the sky caught her attention. She inhaled an awed breath and held it at the sight of an eagle, its wingspan incredibly wide as it soared above the clouds. Unafraid. Majestic. Magnificent.

She had come to Eagle's Landing battered and broken, in need of renewal for her body and a rekindling of her spirit—and she'd found both. Myrna finally knew peace in the knowledge that she had made the right decision for her and Sisi to remain in Hillsdale, feeling as if, indeed, a light did warm her soul.

Everything else still too fresh, too vague, she couldn't think beyond that.

A rustle in the grass made her turn. She looked with surprise to see Dalton a short distance away. Also the victim of a sleepless night, he appeared weary, his eyes rimmed with red, but it was the moisture that sparkled in them that stunned her. There was a vulnerability about his carriage, his expression intent, and she shook her head in confusion.

"Dalton?" Only recently had she allowed herself to say his name when in his exclusive company. Alarm washed through her, and she moved a few steps forward. "It's not Sisi…?"

"Sisi is fine." His voice held a raspy quality, but she barely sounded like herself, either.

"Thank you for staying with me to keep vigil," she said somewhat carefully then realized where he'd found her.

Was that what upset him? "I hope you don't mind that I came here...."

He waved that away and moved toward her, shortening the distance until she could reach out and touch him if she wished.

"I spoke to your cousin. He said you refused him."

"My sister would never have been happy with the life Jeremy had planned. Nor would I. I was foolish not to see that sooner. Thank you for helping me realize that."

He blinked rapidly a few times then swiftly turned, walking toward another grave and bowing his head. She watched his odd behavior.

"I have tried to keep faith for some time," he admitted, his voice so low Myrna almost couldn't hear him. "For weeks I wished to speak, but didn't dare. Too much..." He shook his head. "Too much had happened. I felt the urgency again when we were in the conservatory. To say what's been on my heart, knowing time was my enemy. Later, I resigned myself that the missed opportunity was for the best. You had chosen. I didn't wish you hurt. I resigned myself that it wasn't meant to happen...."

"Dalton...I..." She tried to follow, mystified at his jumble of words, so unlike his usual composed self.

He turned then and looked at her a moment before approaching. He reached for her hands. She freely gave them to him to hold.

"What I'm trying to say, Myrna, is that I love you."

Her heart skipped a beat then quickened. At a loss for breath or speech or thought, she could only stare.

"You are intelligent and beautiful and clever, someone I've come to trust."

"What about Giselle?" She finally found words, wincing at her choice of them but needing to know.

He sobered. "So, you know of Giselle. What have you heard?"

Quietly she told him what little she had learned of the ruptured wedding. "I saw you dance with her at the ball, then you left the room together."

"Giselle and I needed to talk. She's part of the reason I felt unable to speak to you before this. There was a hole in my life that needed mending before I could go on."

She nodded.

"We agreed to reclaim friendship, nothing more. Neither of us would have been happy together, and at last we both acknowledged that. We were lifelong friends, and everyone assumed that someday we would marry. But it was not to be. We had conformed to what our friends and her parents hoped for us instead of what we preferred as individuals. She realized that before I did."

He squeezed her hands, bringing her eyes back to his. "I didn't dare hope that you cared for me, especially once you made the choice to marry your cousin—but then you gave me your father's watch, which you cherished and could never bring yourself to sell. Might I hope that your gift was a look inside your heart and that you return my love, even a little?"

Taking pity on his distress, she nodded. "I do, Dalton, more than *a little*." At the light that suddenly glowed in his fascinating eyes she felt forced to add, "But I cannot be to you what my mother was to *him, the dowager's son.* I'm not like that."

"I would never ask it of you."

Hurt replaced the look of joy on his face, and he released her hands. She missed their warmth.

"Do you truly believe that I have so little respect for you to make such demands or even coax you into such an arrangement?"

"But again I ask, as I did then, *what can there ever be for us?* We admitted how we feel, but that's as far as it can go. I'm only the governess—and not even one with experience. A fraud, really."

"You're not *only* anything, and you're certainly no fraud," he said in frustration.

"It still doesn't change the fact that you're the master of Eagle's Landing, from one of the most prominent families in the county. Much is expected of you. I don't fit in, especially with the added baggage of the scandal of my past."

"It wasn't *your* scandal, and I'll have you know that the Freed men are notorious for not giving a flying fig what others may think."

"Mr. Dalton, sir?"

*"What?"*

Caught up in their altercation, he swiftly turned at the sound of a new voice, his answer coming clipped. Genevieve blinked, looking uncertain whether she wished to speak.

He calmed. "Pardon my brusqueness, Genevieve. What do you want?"

"Mr. Finnegan is here to see you, sir. Says it's urgent."

He let out a prolonged breath. "I hadn't expected him this soon," he said to himself. "Please escort him to the library and tell him I'll join him straightaway. And Genevieve, whatever you may have heard just now goes no further. If I hear even a murmur, I'll know you're the cause and there will be harsh repercussions."

"I didn't hear much, sir. Honest. I only just arrived. Only about the scandal last year, and I won't say another word about what Miss Giselle did." The maid's face turned as red as a persimmon. She gave an awkward bob of a curtsy then hurried back to the house.

Dalton shook his head wearily and turned back to Myrna. "At least she misunderstood and thinks we were talking about *my* past disgrace. I must go and deal with this. Liam Finnegan is my new manager at the mill." She nodded and he studied her eyes, his manner intent. "We *will* speak further, Myrna. That's a promise."

He left her then, not giving her the chance to agree or disagree.

# Chapter 17

"Dalton, dear, whatever is the matter?"

He looked up from the paper at which he'd been staring without seeing and into his mother's concerned eyes.

"I apologize. I was...distracted."

"I think I can guess why," she said with a knowing smile. "This wouldn't have anything to do with a certain young lady who resides in our household, would it?"

"What would cause you to think that?" At the lift of her brows, he surrendered. "Perhaps."

"It isn't difficult to see. She behaves in the same manner, with her mind in the clouds and that same uncertainty I see clouding your expression. You would think that her agreement to stay in Hillsdale four days ago would have produced a different reaction." She chuckled.

"I love her, Mother." He decided to admit everything.

"I suspected as much.... And?" she added when he didn't respond.

"Some of the points she brought up when I professed my

feelings have made me hesitant to speak, once I thought about what she said. They were the same points Giselle made, of why she couldn't marry me."

"Myrna and Giselle are nothing alike."

"I know that." Frustrated, he set his quill down and leaned back in the chair. "But they both made it clear that they felt as if they wouldn't fit in with our family."

"It's that serious, then?" she queried softly. "You care for her that much?"

"Yes. But I don't know how to proceed."

"Did you propose?"

He glumly shook his head. "After the debacle with Giselle, I'm somewhat apprehensive to do so, only to have her reject me. Worse, have her accept, then later run away." He laughed without humor. "She has a habit of doing that. Running. In a sense, she was running the night we met on the train."

"You must tell her how you feel, Dalton. The heart can be tricky, but it's faithful when love is true. If Giselle had loved you enough, our status in the community would never have prompted her rash decision to flee. Instead, it became the excuse she needed to make that choice. I sense something entirely different with Myrna."

"Yes?"

"Yes." She smiled mysteriously. "But you must find out for yourself."

"It always comes down to choices, doesn't it?" he stated dryly, his gaze going to the cold hearth. The image of him with her there, wiping her tears and the tender kiss that followed provoked his memory.

"Life is full of choices, and as soon as one is made another comes to take its place. You made the choice to tackle the family business, with none of the training your brother had, and you've done well. Now it's time to confront matters of the heart with that same perseverance.

That, or resign yourself to live an empty life without the woman you love beside you."

He winced. "You never mince words, do you, Mother?"

"Of course not. What would be the point?"

She began to walk away then seemed to think twice and looked back. "That said, I should tell you—she might not be with us much longer. You've been so busy with business affairs, you refused to take dinner with us—well, that's the excuse you gave at any rate. But last night she told me she might be seeking work as a laundress at the hotel."

"What?" His entire body snapped to attention. "Why would she do that when she has a perfectly good place here, with us?"

"Perhaps you should ask her that. Especially after your declaration to her."

"Then you approve?" he asked quietly.

She smiled. "I already think of her as a daughter."

She opened the door and pivoted as another thought occurred. "Would you mind going in search of the girls and telling them to come back to the house? They're at the pond. It looks like it might rain, and it wouldn't do for Sisi to get wet so soon after her recent scare. The walk might help to clear your head."

"Of course." Dalton rose from his chair. "No need to convince me."

Only when he arrived at the spot did Dalton realize he had again been manipulated by his cunning mother. The girls were nowhere in sight.

But Myrna stood in the small gazebo, facing the pond. At the sound of his step, she turned. A wary expression lit her eyes as they stared at one another, and Dalton knew the time had come for candid discussion, no matter the outcome.

The moment Sisi begged Myrna to accompany her to visit the ducks, she should have been suspicious—doubly so when Rebecca appeared shortly after they arrived and told Sisi that her nana wished to see them both. The girls had then run off before Myrna could draw breath to ask questions.

Now, upon seeing Dalton for the first time in four days, Myrna understood. It didn't help the state of her emotional equilibrium that she'd just been thinking about him, wondering why he'd been avoiding her, before she turned and saw him standing there.

"Hello." He seemed tense. "The girls aren't here, are they? Mother asked me to fetch them."

"They were." She offered a faint, amused smile. "For under ten seconds. Rebecca said that your mother wanted to talk with both girls."

"Ah, I see." He nodded as if not surprised. "It seems we've been hoodwinked once again."

*But why was there a need?* she wanted to demand. And she wondered if he regretted professing his feelings to her. She should just go and never look back.

"I should return before I'm missed." Even as she said the words, droplets struck all around, and Dalton moved into the gazebo.

"You have no parasol. It's likely a brief shower, like the one yesterday. The clouds aren't that dark."

She didn't mention that she had never owned a parasol, uncertain of exactly what to say.

He moved to the rail to look out over the pond where two ducks glided on the surface of the water now pebbled with raindrops.

"I've been meaning to speak with you…."

Four days she had wished for this moment. Now all she wanted was to escape it.

"You don't need to. I understand," she whispered, and he turned his head to look at her. "We were both weary from lack of sleep. You spoke in haste—"

He looked at her in confusion. "I meant every word I said."

She stared in surprise. "Oh."

"Did you?"

She hesitated. "Which part?"

"All of it."

"Yes," she finally admitted.

He pivoted to face her. "Then why are you again thinking of leaving us? Are you unhappy here?" Misery clouded his eyes.

"No," she hastened to reassure him. "I love your home. It's peaceful. You and your mother have made me feel like a member of the family—"

"Then why on God's green earth do you want to move into town and become *a laundress?*"

"I *can't* live here anymore. Not feeling as I do!"

"You're talking in riddles, woman," he said, perplexed. "You told me you care for me, is that not so?" His eyes sought hers for an answer and she gave a little nod. "You admitted to loving it here, you feel like part of the family. What am I missing?"

"I'm not like my mother, nor will I ever be."

"I told you, I would never ask that of you, and I wish you would stop bringing it up."

"But I have no desire even to entertain the temptation," she barely whispered, shocked that she was speaking so forthrightly, but there must be no misunderstandings between them, and clearly there were. "Staying on here, as the governess—"

"You don't have to be the governess."

"What would I be, then?"

He hesitated. "Before I answer, why do you feel that you don't fit in? It makes no sense, with what you just said."

She should never have admitted her feelings to him.

"Your friends don't think so. The town sure doesn't. At

the ball, a few acted differently toward me when they found out I was the hired help and not a true guest."

"Then they are pigheaded fools," he scoffed. "Am I to cater to the whims of the populace or my associates when it comes to my personal affairs?"

She held her breath. "What do you mean?"

"I mean that in my estimation you fit perfectly. With me."

He took her hand in his and slowly knelt to one knee. Her eyes widened while her heart skipped a beat then raced at the sudden realization of what he was doing.

"Do you not know that I consider you one of the most amazing women I've ever met? With a heart and soul that are pure, despite all you've suffered. You strive to do what's right, always putting others first. You are fiercely loyal to those you love. And I would consider it a privilege if you would stay with me. Not as my mistress, Myrna— but as my wife."

Everything seemed to freeze within and without; she could produce no words. When she could speak, they weren't the words she wished to say.

"What of your feelings for Giselle? Do you no longer love her?"

He drew his brows together at her whisper. "While it's true that Giselle and I have mended our differences, in all honesty, I never felt as strongly about her as I've come to feel about you. A love so deep, it hurts when you're not near."

She brought the hand he wasn't holding to her mouth in an attempt to quench a soft sob. She understood such words. She felt it, too.

Gently he turned her other hand over in his, fingering her mother's ring. "That is why I've remained silent. Giselle told me some of the same things you did—that she didn't feel she fit in, that the idea of marriage to me had become a trap, and it worried me that you also felt that way—until five minutes ago, when you admitted you were happy with us and loved it here."

At the recollection of Dalton left jilted at the altar and the realization of how difficult this must be for him, her heart ached in sympathy, even while she felt she might float away with bliss to hear him speak.

"As you've been open with me, so I want to be with you," she said. "I don't want you to come to feel the way she did. About me. Thinking marriage to me a trap or that I don't fit in. Not too long ago you thought me a woman of questionable character."

"I won't." His words were firm, his eyes sincere. "And those days are long in the past."

"Speaking of the past, what of my family's scandal?" she sadly reminded him.

"It shouldn't be yours to bear!"

"But it is. We can't change history, Dalton. And once before, someone from the past found me and caused heartache. Should that again happen, I don't wish to be a burden to you or your mother. I don't wish for my scandal to become yours."

He swiftly brought her hand to his lips and kissed her fingers then again looked up at her. "You alone have borne the weight of your family's secret far too long. Now I *want* to be there for you. If that day should come and the past resurfaces, then together we'll face whatever snakes lie in wait. We Freeds can be a formidable lot. We take care of our own." His gentle teasing soothed her fears. Again he stroked her mother's band. "Let me replace this ring that ties you to your past with another, one that symbolizes the future I wish to give you. You have my heart, dearest Myrna. Will you give me yours in return?"

The tears slipped from her eyes while the light rain continued to fall outside their shelter.

"I so desperately want to believe you," she whispered, a lifetime of old fear difficult to suppress, even with the promise of all she desired.

"I would *never* hurt you. I'd sooner cut off my hand. If you cannot yet trust me, will you at least trust that?"

"Yes," she said without reservation. "You're a wonderful man, Dalton. I was wrong to ever think otherwise. I do trust you. And…and if you truly wish it of me, then I would be most honored to marry you."

His eyes brightened. "I do wish it, with all that I am." He stood and cradled her face between his hands, but instead of sweeping her into his passionate embrace as had been her experience twice, he stopped short of doing so. "I should like to kiss you."

His words held the hint of a question, and her smile trembled with happiness.

"I should like your kiss."

He smiled, his lips brushing hers, this kiss not tentative like the first, nor as desperate as their last, but tender and undemanding, full of the promise of forever he had just conveyed. In the powerful circle of his arms she felt warmed to her very marrow, as if she'd finally found safe haven after searching so long. When he pulled away, she shivered to lose such closeness.

"You're cold," he said in a self-chastising manner. "How thoughtless of me not to give you my coat." He gave no heed to her mild protests, unbuttoning his waistcoat and slipping it around her shoulders. She drew his coat even closer at the sensation of heat from his body that lingered on the silk lining and warmed her flesh.

"There seems to be a lull." He looked at the sky. "Shall we make a run for it?"

His eyes were alight with boyish charm, a quality about him she only recently noticed in past weeks, and she giggled like a schoolgirl and nodded. Despite the dismal clouds she felt as if sunbeams had burst to life and danced within her soul.

"Together?" He held out his hand.

She took it, pulling his waistcoat over her head with the other. "Together."

They raced for the manor, the storm in their lives at last subsided, the downpour over the countryside now a light, drizzling mist. Myrna smiled to know that she would never again face the future alone—no longer cold, stark, perilous or uncertain.

She had found the courage to confront it....

And a reason to believe.

# Epilogue

*Two years later*

"Sisi, my pet, will you hand me the blanket?"

Myrna held her hand out for the snowy white cloth. Like the doting little aunt she'd become, Sisi picked it up from the ground where it had slipped and tucked the folds around her niece, fussing over her.

"Hello, Lila Jane," Sisi cooed when the baby sleepily opened her eyes, a shade between her mother's green and her father's blue. Myrna hid a smile to recall her conversation of two months ago. Lila had been his grandmother's name, and Dalton's mother had expressed delight that they'd chosen it. Lila was Dalton's wish, but Jane had been Myrna's choice.

"Someone in your family?" Dalton had inquired.

"You might say that." She wondered what he would say if he learned she had named their child after a fictional heroine, the novel now a favorite. In part she had done so because she shared many traits that Jane Eyre possessed, along with her triumph to gain the love of the master of the household whom she had come to cherish—and tonight, perhaps during their nightly stroll, she might tell him why. She giggled to think of what he would say if she admitted how she once compared him to the formidable Mr. Rochester.

The months leading up to their spring wedding had been a blur for Myrna. Mother Freed had shown delight to gain Myrna as her daughter-in-law, and Myrna deemed it only proper that she confess her family's scandal. To Myrna's relief, Dalton's mother had been reassuring, as well as insistent that no prospective daughter-in-law of hers would stay at a public boardinghouse. So Myrna had remained at Eagle's Landing.

Overnight, Mother Freed became a strict if devoted chaperone with two eager aides. It was rare that Dalton stole a kiss that Myrna was only too happy to give, before his mother or one or both girls would appear. Their moments alone grew rare and brief, the reason a source of much shared amusement between them. Her nightly strolls with Dalton were restricted to daytime with both girls in attendance and resumed only after their sweet chapel wedding.

Myrna had wished to keep the ceremony simple, but Mother Freed wanted to invite the entire town. They reached a compromise and invited all the quaint chapel could hold. At the ensuing party, many others from all over the county arrived at the manor to wish them well, including Giselle, who warmly took Myrna's hands in hers and wished her every happiness. Myrna had been uncertain how she would respond to meeting Dalton's former fiancée, but at the sincere kindness in the woman's dark eyes, she felt reassured. Since then, she and Giselle had become friends.

Myrna and her new husband had honeymooned in Europe, exploring its many ancient castles and indulging in the legend and lore.

A month after their return, Myrna's shy announcement of a baby sent the household into a flurry of excitement, and the maids prepared a room for the nursery, close to the master bedchamber. Most surprising to Myrna, the lock on the old playroom disappeared, the room still consigned to storage but no longer forbidden, and to the little girls' delight, the replica dollhouse of Eagle's Landing appeared on Christmas morning in their play area.

"It's what Alyssa would have wanted," Dalton said quietly to Myrna while watching their young charges play together, a bittersweet smile on his face.

So much healing had occurred in the more than two years since Myrna arrived. She had learned that trust, even justly deserved, took time to cultivate and must be nurtured, each opportunity golden, never to be taken for granted or ignored. Since their daughter had come to bless their lives, the ghostly weeping was never again heard by the maids late in the night, the owner of the creaking rocker too content to dote on her granddaughter to dwell on past losses.

"Dalton," Sisi squealed, breaking into Myrna's thoughts. She watched her sister run across the lawn to him to be scooped up into his embrace. "Lila Jane smiled today!"

"Did she?" He carried his little sister-in-law to where Myrna sat in the shade of the summer's afternoon.

"Uh-huh. She must be happy to be here."

"Did you doubt it?" he teased.

"No, this is the best place ever!"

Myrna's heart gave a little jump as it always did to see him, then another when their eyes met and held in that intimate manner that made her breathless. Life with Dalton had indeed exceeded her fondest dreams and trounced all her old qualms.

"And how are my other two girls?" He set Sisi on the ground and bent to kiss Myrna's temple then brushed his finger along the baby's cheek.

Before she could assure him they were well, they heard the sound of a foot being stomped.

"What about me?" Rebecca insisted with a pout. "Am I no longer one of your girls?"

Dalton chuckled, he and Myrna sharing an amused glance at Rebecca's customary dramatics, before he whirled and scooped up their niece causing her to squeal and giggle a protest when he tickled her ribs.

"You most certainly are, young miss! Don't you forget it."

Reassured, Rebecca smiled and took Sisi's hand once he set her down. The two ran toward the pond.

"Don't stay away long," Myrna called out. "Dinner is in less than an hour."

"We won't," Rebecca called back. "We just want to see the baby ducks!"

Dalton retraced his steps to Myrna's side. "Which means I shall likely have to fetch them within the hour."

Myrna smiled in agreement. "How did things go in town?"

"Tonight, during our stroll, we can talk about the day's affairs," he said, lowering his body so that their eyes were level. He slipped his hand against her head, cradling it and turning her face toward him. "To find ourselves alone after having missed your presence all day and eagerly counting the minutes when I may again return to you, I cannot help but take advantage of this moment."

With that he kissed her, gentle and slow but no less passionate, and she returned his affection with as much fervor that a woman holding a sleeping infant could possess.

"I am fortunate to have taken the train that night two years ago, instead of the one earlier in the day as I intended," he said once he pulled back to look into her eyes.

"What prevented you?" she asked at this previously unknown morsel of information.

"I overslept," he admitted with a sheepish grin.

She giggled at that. Dalton was no cheerful greeter of the dawn. She discovered that juicy tidbit the morning after they were wed and often enjoyed devising methods to rouse him, some loving, some mischievous, even tickling his ribs as he'd done with Rebecca—her every attempt always ending with success and with her in his arms.

"Please don't tell me I owe this moment and every one we have shared to your slothfulness to greet the sunrise?" she mused in mock chastisement but knew she owed their meeting to a far worthier source.

He laughed, his eyes sparkling with mirth. "It behooves me to say it, but alas, it is so."

"There are far worse traits, I suppose." She grinned. "No matter. I love you for all that you are, Dalton Freed."

She could never express such words enough.

"As I shall always love you, my dearest Myrna."

And she would never tire of hearing such words.

Each day she thanked God for bringing them together, that in the loss of tragedy she found the miracle of happiness. In all storms they since faced, they had done so together. They struggled, they learned, and always they loved, and Myrna truly felt as if she soared with the eagles at Eagle's Landing.

Or perhaps it was her unwavering faith that made her so lighthearted?

\* \* \* \* \*

# REQUEST YOUR FREE BOOKS!

## 2 FREE INSPIRATIONAL NOVELS
## PLUS 2
## FREE
## MYSTERY GIFTS

*Love Inspired*

**YES!** Please send me 2 FREE Love Inspired® novels and my 2 FREE mystery gifts (gifts are worth about $10). After receiving them, if I don't wish to receive any more books, I can return the shipping statement marked "cancel." If I don't cancel, I will receive 6 brand-new novels every month and be billed just $4.74 per book in the U.S. or $5.24 per book in Canada. That's a savings of at least 21% off the cover price. It's quite a bargain! Shipping and handling is just 50¢ per book in the U.S. and 75¢ per book in Canada.* I understand that accepting the 2 free books and gifts places me under no obligation to buy anything. I can always return a shipment and cancel at any time. Even if I never buy another book, the two free books and gifts are mine to keep forever.

105/305 IDN F49N

| Name | (PLEASE PRINT) | |
|------|------|------|

| Address | | Apt. # |
|------|------|------|

| City | State/Prov. | Zip/Postal Code |
|------|------|------|

Signature (if under 18, a parent or guardian must sign)

### Mail to the **Harlequin® Reader Service:**
**IN U.S.A.:** P.O. Box 1867, Buffalo, NY 14240-1867
**IN CANADA:** P.O. Box 609, Fort Erie, Ontario L2A 5X3

**Are you a subscriber to Love Inspired books
and want to receive the larger-print edition?
Call 1-800-873-8635 or visit www.ReaderService.com.**

* Terms and prices subject to change without notice. Prices do not include applicable taxes. Sales tax applicable in N.Y. Canadian residents will be charged applicable taxes. Offer not valid in Quebec. This offer is limited to one order per household. Not valid for current subscribers to Love Inspired books. All orders subject to credit approval. Credit or debit balances in a customer's account(s) may be offset by any other outstanding balance owed by or to the customer. Please allow 4 to 6 weeks for delivery. Offer available while quantities last.

**Your Privacy**—The Harlequin® Reader Service is committed to protecting your privacy. Our Privacy Policy is available online at www.ReaderService.com or upon request from the Harlequin Reader Service.
We make a portion of our mailing list available to reputable third parties that offer products we believe may interest you. If you prefer that we not exchange your name with third parties, or if you wish to clarify or modify your communication preferences, please visit us at www.ReaderService.com/consumerschoice or write to us at Harlequin Reader Service Preference Service, P.O. Box 9062, Buffalo, NY 14269. Include your complete name and address.

LIDIR13R

# *ReaderService*.com

## Manage your account online!

- Review your order history
- Manage your payments
- Update your address

> ### We've designed
> ### the Harlequin® Reader Service
> ### website just for you.

## Enjoy all the features!

- Reader excerpts from any series
- Respond to mailings and special monthly offers
- Discover new series available to you
- Browse the Bonus Bucks catalog
- Share your feedback

*Visit us at:*

# ReaderService.com